I0460319

Shattered
Dreams

The Man in Blue

By
R.W.K. Clark

Copyright © 2016 R.W.K. Clark
All rights reserved, www.rwkclark.com
r@rwkclark.com

This is a work of fiction. All names, characters, locales, and incidents are
the product of the author's imagination and any resemblance to actual
people, places or events is coincidental or fictionalized.
Published in the United States by Clarkltd.
Po Box 45313 Rio Rancho, NM 87174
info@clarkltd.com

Edition 1

United States Copyright Office
#TX 8-345-118 August 2016
Library of Congress Control Number: 2017907159
International Standard Book Numbers
ISBN-10: 0997876719
ISBN-13: 978-0997876710
ASIN: B01K8U3J9K

/200801

CONTENTS

ACKNOWLEDGMENTS

I dedicate this novel to my wonderful readers and for all the amazing people I've met and those I haven't. To my family and loved ones, all your support will not be forgotten.

This book was made possible by reviews from readers like you.

Thank you

R.W.K. Clark

CHAPTER 1

Henry James O'Brien sat on the rough orange living room carpet with his face tilted upward. His full attention was on the old nineteen-inch television before him, and his eyes and ears were giving their all to the images on the screen and the words the characters were speaking. When he was watching his shows, it was nearly impossible to break the reverie he would inevitably be in.

"Jimmy," his mother said from the small kitchen, her voice slightly raised so the boy could hear her over the program he was viewing. It didn't matter, though; the people her son was watching were the only ones he was hearing.

Luciana O'Brien walked to the kitchen door and gazed out into the tiny living room at her son. His back was to her, and the room was growing dim as the sun began to tuck itself away for the day. Only the light from the picture tube allowed her to see his face, even in the slightest. She smiled to herself: what a beautiful face it was.

Luciana stood there, simply enjoying the moment. She was gone from him so often, what with one full-time job and another on a part-time basis. She tended to take advantage of all the little moments she could get with him. Jimmy was six years old now, and he would be seven in only two months. Soon she would blink, and he would be a grown man, ready to leave home and start a life on his own. She felt as if time was slipping away from her too quickly already.

"Jimmy, it's time for your supper." Luciana's feminine voice was thick with an Italian accent, and it was a sound Jimmy loved. This time it caught his attention, and the boy turned to her with his eyes alight.

A smile crept over his face when he saw that she too was smiling. "What did you make, Mommy?"

"Hmmm," she replied mysteriously. Luciana crossed her arms over her chest and began to walk slowly in his direction. She appeared to be withholding some great mystery about the meal from him, but he knew she was only playing. This was a regular game between the two of them. "I thought you asked me to prepare your favorite: liver and onions. Delicioso!"

Now the boy threw himself backward onto the carpet dramatically. He rolled his eyes and whined with great theatrics. "No, Mommy! Ugh! Oh, no!"

He knew good and well that his mother didn't ever make liver, just as she knew that her son despised it. Jimmy's father, Henry, had grown up eating the dish frequently because his parents loved it. On several occasions, his father's mother had prepared it for little Jimmy when she had come for a visit, and it had been all the boy could do just to get it down without being sick. But he had always been more concerned about his grandmother's feelings than his own distaste for the meat, and he struggled through it successfully every time. Now it was an affectionate joke between mother and son. His grandmother no longer visited, and he no longer worried about the disgusting meat-like substance. It was a relief because Jimmy knew he could go the rest of his life without eating it.

Luciana dropped to her knees on the floor next to him and began to tickle him with fervor. Jimmy's laughter erupted so strongly that it took over his entire being, and he couldn't even struggle against her fingertips. Luciana herself had difficulty keeping herself from laughing and losing control.

"But you'll eat it like a good boy, won't you?" she asked, a large, toothy smile on her face. "Won't you, my little one? Yes? Yes?"

"No, Mommy! No!" Jimmy squirmed and laughed until tears ran down his face and he was completely out of breath. At last, his mother stopped the tickling and sat back on her behind, overcome with laughter herself. After a moment they were both sighing as they tried to breathe, with Jimmy wiping the tears from his cheeks.

"Oh, Jimmy," Luciana said finally. "You are so much fun. Would it make you feel better if I told you we are having spaghetti? Spaghetti with garlic toast?"

Once again the boy dove into his classic histrionic behavior. "Thank the Lord!" He threw his arm over his face as if he never thought he would be rescued from the punishment of liver. "Yes, Mommy. You know that!"

Luciana stood and took her son by both his hands and helped him to his feet. "What are you watching?" she asked as they walked to the kitchen.

"*Men in Blue*," Jimmy replied. "It's my favorite, you know?"

Luciana nodded and pulled out Jimmy's chair. "I do. What is the program about tonight?"

She began to dish up their plates, piling spaghetti on first, then adding green beans and a slice of garlic toast to each as he related the details of that evening's episode. "Tonight Captain Steele found out one of the bad cops has been the boss of a club of robbers. The robbers have been stealing from old people because the old people couldn't fight for themselves. I think people like that are the very worst in the entire world. Isn't that so bad, Mommy?"

She put his plate and a small glass of cold milk in front of him, then grabbed her own from the counter and took the chair across from him at the tiny two-person kitchen table. "Yes, Jimmy. It is horrible to steal, and it is worse to hurt those who are weak just because you can."

The boy stuffed a forkful of spaghetti into his mouth, and as he chewed, a faraway look came over his face. Luciana watched him as she ate, her heart swelling with such love she thought she may die from it. "What are you thinking about, Jimmy O'Brien?"

He swallowed and took a drink of milk. "I hate the bad guys, Mommy. I wish there were no bad guys anywhere, ever! What would we all do without police?"

"It would be a very dangerous world, wouldn't it, my love?"

Jimmy nodded and took another bite, so Luciana followed suit. After he had swallowed yet again, he said, "Someday I want to be a policeman. I'm gonna help keep people safe, and I'm gonna help get rid of the bad guys, Mommy."

Her smile faded, but Jimmy didn't notice. "I think you would make the best policeman ever, Henry James O'Brien. The very best! There is not a doubt of that in my mind at all."

The two ate the rest of their meal in overall silence, only chatting briefly about Jimmy's first-grade class and Luciana's part-time job at the laundry. Otherwise, they both reveled in the feel of each other's presence, and they enjoyed having each other's company.

∞

Luciana silently opened Jimmy's bedroom door and crept in, using only the dim light from his tiny nightlight to see her way through the room. When she reached his bed, she bent over and looked at his face. She so badly wanted to run her fingers through his sandy-brown hair and feel its softness, but Jimmy had always been a light sleeper, and it was late. It wouldn't do to cause him to lose even the smallest amount of sleep; he had class tomorrow after all.

Instead, she put her nose to his head and inhaled. She could smell the fresh, clean scent of the shampoo she had used to clean his hair before bed, and it made her smile. She looked at him once again, and satisfied that he was fine she left his room, softly closing the door behind her.

Luciana spent the next half-hour on her knees next to her bed, praying for her son. She also prayed for the children in the world who had no one to love them, and those who had no home and no food. She prayed for the elderly and the grieving. She prayed for the strength to continue her job at the laundry, and she was thankful for it, even though she hated it with all that was in her. She prayed for her boss that he would be happy in his marriage and stop touching her and flirting with her. Finally, she prayed for her ex-husband and the woman he was now with, the woman he had left her and Jimmy to be with. Luciana prayed that he would have happiness.

Something inside of her told her with certainty that someday, when he was a grown man, Jimmy was, going to be a policeman, just as he wanted to. The thought terrified her, but she knew that he was a good boy through and through. If anyone would make the perfect policeman, it would be her wonderful, soft-hearted Henry James.

Finally, she crossed her chest and kissed the rosary she held lovingly in her hand. She stood and put the rosary and her Bible safely into her nightstand drawer, then she climbed under the blankets on her bed. She was exhausted, and within minutes she was sleeping like a baby, dreaming dreams of cops with Jimmy's face.

CHAPTER 2

"I'm gonna be the bank robber!"

Kevin Marshall, Brad Fuller, and Jimmy were on the playground for their afternoon recess. As usual, the trio were preparing to play Cops and Robbers, something they did every day, even on the weekends. For each of the two recess periods during the school day, they would meet at the jungle gym, and from there they would run off, separating themselves from all the other kids on the playground. Jimmy liked it that way because sometimes they would argue about who gets to be what, and if a spat started, it always seemed to send some little tattletale to the supervising teacher.

Most of the time Brad and Kevin would insist on being the robbers, and Jimmy was fine with that. The last thing he wanted to be was a low-down, dirty crook. While the other boys found it cool and appealing, Jimmy found it to be sickening. He knew it was only make-believe, but even if it was, who wanted to be a person that hurt other people?

Sometimes Kevin would put up a fight about their roles. Brad was nearly always happy to be the sneering criminal, and mostly Kevin was as well, but about once a week, he would demand to be the cop. Jimmy thought that he did this only to be difficult. He did it only when he was having a bad day, or when his mommy and daddy had been fighting the night before, which seemed to happen about once a week. When Kevin made this demand, Jimmy wouldn't argue with his friend; all he would do was suggest that they be 'partners,' and that both of them could catch Brad, the 'mastermind.'

Today proved to be one of the easy-going days, and for the first fifteen minutes of their recess break, Kevin and Brad pretended to rob a store with a couple of big guns while Jimmy pursued them in a valiant effort to save the store, its elderly owners, and all of their hard earned money. When it came time for the chase, he went after them with a pointed finger, and he yelled, "Freeze! Put your hands in the air!"

The two boys dropped to the ground just as a stern voice came from behind them. "Kevin Marshall!"

The kids turned around, startled. It was Mrs. Edwards, the playground supervising teacher that day. Kevin jumped to his feet, a nervous look in his eyes.

"What?" he asked her, his feet shuffling nervously.

Mrs. Edwards approached them quickly and bent down to Kevin's level when she reached him. "Mrs. Schulte just came out from the building and asked me to send you into her. What do you suppose this could be about, Mr. Marshall? I'm pretty sure you know, and I certainly don't have to tell you, do I?" The teacher's foot was tapping, and she had an angry look in her eyes.

Kevin looked down at his feet and began to push a

rock with his toe. Jimmy could tell by the look on his playmate's face that the boy knew exactly what she was referring to, but he wasn't going to give up any information. He shrugged without making eye contact.

"I don't know," he said in a low voice.

Mrs. Edwards stood up straight and crossed her arms over her chest, her foot still tapping away. "You don't know anything about Emily Preston's missing money, young man? Mrs. Schulte says you were in Emily's desk before the break, and when she confronted you on it, you told her you were putting a pencil back that you had borrowed." The teacher glanced at the other two young men before continuing. "Emily went back to the classroom to get her marbles from her desk, and her money was missing." She turned to Brad and Jimmy. "I think it would be in the best interest of both of you to find someone else to play with at recess. Anyone hanging around with this young man is going to end up seeing nothing but trouble, both now and in the future!"

Now Kevin looked at the woman with defiance. "I didn't take no darn money!"

"Well, I think you should come with me right now, and we will just see if that is true or false. We will check your person and your locker and desk. If you did take it, we would certainly find it! Mrs. Schulte is waiting with Emily right over there." She pointed at the teacher and the girl before taking Kevin by the arm. "If you didn't take it, you won't mind turning out your pockets and proving it." She began to walk away with the boy, who was resisting her at every step. "You two can carry on; don't you worry yourselves with this little… misfit!"

Jimmy and Brad watched as Mrs. Edwards led their playmate away toward Mrs. Schulte and Emily Preston by the collar of his shirt. He had a sneer on his face and resisted her entirely. After a moment, Brad said, "Why would he take money, especially from a girl?"

Jimmy felt himself burning with anger. "We should never take money, not from anyone, if it isn't ours."

Brad turned to him. "Do you want to keep playing?"

With a shake of the head, Jimmy O'Brien said, "Nah. And I don't think I wanna play with Kevin anymore, either." He began to walk away from Brad, but the boy jogged to catch up with him.

"Wait up!" When he caught Jimmy, he said, "What's the matter, Jimmy? Why don't you wanna play with Kevin anymore?"

Jimmy stopped in his tracks, but he didn't answer his friend right away. Instead, he watched from a distance as the two teachers, Schulte and Edwards, stood with confrontational poses before Kevin Marshall. Jimmy's face remained angry and obstinate, and though he could not hear what was being said, he knew the boy was getting a good cussing. Next, they must have told him to turn out his pockets because he suddenly took a step back away from them with panic on his face. Mrs. Edwards took Kevin by the arm, and Mrs. Schulte began to go through the pockets of his jeans herself.

In only moments, the teacher withdrew something and shook it in the boy's face. He only looked at the ground and pretended to ignore her while Emily Preston looked on, wiping her tears with relief. Jimmy O'Brien felt sick to his stomach.

He turned to Brad and shook his head. "You know, when we play Cops and Robbers someone has to be the bad guy, Brad, or else, we can't play the game. But I don't want to be the bad guy ever, even when we are playing. Why do you?"

Brad shrugged, and a thoughtful look came over his face. "I guess because when you pretend to be the bad guy, you get to do stuff that looks exciting on TV, and really, you would never want to do stuff like that in real life. Only bad people do, so you just pretend."

Jimmy turned back to see Kevin being led through the playground door back into the school. "Well, I don't want to do the things bad guys do. They hurt people. They make them cry, and they don't care, and they even seem to like it. The truth is, I don't want to even be friends with bad guys, and Kevin just showed us he is a bad guy. He stole from Emily, and then he even lied to a teacher about it just so he wouldn't get into trouble. The teacher was right: hanging out with him is going to bring us nothing but trouble in the end."

The two boys started walking again, heading toward the building themselves. Soon Mrs. Edwards would blow the whistle to signal the end of recess, so there was no point in dawdling. Brad stopped once more, though, and touched Jimmy on the arm.

"But sometimes Kevin wants to be the cop," he said. "What about that?"

Now it was Jimmy's turn to consider. "Maybe it's so he can be bad to people without getting caught, or maybe it's just to make him feel better about being bad. Either way, I don't wanna be his friend anymore." He turned to Brad and offered him a consoling smile and a pat on the back. "We're the good guys in real life though, Brad. Just keep being the good guy; that's all that matters."

With that, the two boys continued back to the school building just as the whistle blew.

CHAPTER 3

Jimmy slid his key into the lock on the apartment door. His mother worked full-time, Monday through Friday, until 4:30 in the afternoon; he was always home at four. He was used to coming home to a silent, empty home, but he didn't mind. It gave him time to watch the four o'clock rerun of *Men in Blue*.

He locked the door behind him, just as his mother had taught him, then he flipped the television on before grabbing two cookies from the jar on the kitchen counter. His mother didn't want him to have any more because she didn't want him to ruin his supper. He never wanted to hurt her or damage her trust in him, so he obeyed her directives without question. He knew in his heart that his mother wanted only what was best for him.

As he sat on the couch eating his cookies and waiting for the show to start, he thought of his mother. She was always so tired. She would come home and they would eat their supper together, always homemade, and always delicious. Then, on weekday evenings only, she would leave at six-thirty for her part-time job at the laundry down the block. She did dry cleaning until ten-thirty, and she was always home by eleven. He couldn't wait to grow up and become a cop for real; that was when he would take care of her and all her needs, just like his father never had.

His program began, and Jimmy jumped up from the couch and sat in his spot on the floor, directly in front of the TV set. A smile of anticipation was plastered on his face, and his eyes were lit up with joy as he waited to see what episode would be playing. He had seen nearly every single one he would bet, and some of them two or three times, but he never grew tired of watching Captain Steele and the boys get the bad guys off the street.

When he grew up, he was going to work hard and concentrate on being the best cop the world had ever seen. He was going to be honest, and trustworthy, just like Captain Steele. Everyone would love him, just like on the show, because his heart was pure and made of gold, and he made everyone feel safe, just like Captain Steele.

Jimmy put his last cookie on the floor next to him and began to clap with elation as the show began. It was only a minute in, and he knew exactly what episode it was: it was the one with a homeless man who sleeps on a bench. He gets accused of hurting an old lady in a bad, bad way, and they throw him in jail. But Captain Steele talks to him, and he believes the man is innocent. Captain Steele works hard and finds the real culprit, then he helps the homeless man by getting him a job in his brother's factory. It was an awesome episode! Jimmy began to recite the actors' lines right along with them, even enunciating in all the right spots.

So awesome was it, in fact, that Jimmy lost track of time. Soon Luciana's key could be heard in the door, and even though his subconscious registered the sound he was powerless to do any more than spit out, "Hi, Mommy!"

She put her purse on the small table next to the door and turned to her son. She grinned from ear to ear as she saw the excitement and enthusiasm in his eyes. He did not have his father to look up to; at least he chose men with integrity to emulate and love, even if it was only television. He could have been like other kids that admired gangsters. No, she wouldn't complain. Jimmy was a good boy through and through.

"Is it a good one today?" she asked as she strode next to him and looked down at the set.

Jimmy nodded vigorously. "Yep! It's the best one ever!"

Luciana had to stop herself from laughing out loud; he said that every day, about every episode. "Well, I'm going to start supper. You can tell me all about it when we eat."

She went into the kitchen and took a package of two thawed chicken thighs out of the refrigerator, then grabbed a couple of brown potatoes from a bottom cupboard door. Next, she fished a can of corn from another cupboard with a grimace. She hated feeding Jimmy canned vegetables, but it was all she could afford at the time. She put the can down and set about preparing their meal. The sound of the television and her son's voice from the other room made her feel as though all of the things she did daily, all of her sacrifices, were more than worth it.

In the living room, Jimmy sat back in disgust as a commercial for beer came on the television. He popped the rest of his cookie in his mouth and chewed it while he hummed the theme song to *Men in Blue*. Just then the telephone rang.

Jimmy jumped up, eager to help his mother out. "I've got it, Mommy!" He sped over to the end table and picked up the receiver, and with his politest voice said, "Hello! O'Brien's!"

There was a brief pause on the other end. "Hello?" Jimmy repeated.

"Jimmy! How are you doing, son? How are you?"

Jimmy's brow knit for a moment in confusion. It was a familiar voice, but he couldn't place it. "May I ask who's calling, please?"

After another pause, the man said, "Jimmy, it's Daddy. You don't know my voice?"

Jimmy's stomach instantly roiled with nervous anxiety. "Oh. I'm sorry father. I guess I was distracted. Hold on, and I'll get Mommy." He wasn't aware of how cold his voice was toward the man, but Henry O'Brien certainly wasn't oblivious to the fact. The truth was, however, that he didn't really care.

He quickly set the receiver down on the table and looked at it as if it were a snake. Not only did he not recognize the voice, he barely knew the man. What he did know was that he had left him and his Mommy when they needed him the most, so he certainly didn't want to talk to him. He never really had any interest in his father at all. He and his Mommy were happy without him, so who needed him?

Jimmy walked to the kitchen slowly. Maybe he would lose his patience and hang up. When he got to the kitchen, he peeked in the door. "Father is on the phone."

Luciana turned to her son with wide eyes. "Are you sure?"

Jimmy nodded.

"What does he want? Did he say?"

"No," he replicd. "I didn't want to talk to him, so I just came to get you."

Luciana nodded and smoothed her apron before following him into the living room. Jimmy turned the television down so his mother could hear, then he pretended to watch it while he listened to his mother's side of the conversation. He wanted to make sure his father didn't make her cry. If he did, Jimmy would get on that phone and give him a piece of his mind, alright. He would tell that guy to leave them alone and never call them again. He hated for his mother to cry, and he didn't have time for anyone that caused it.

"Hello, Henry?" His mother seemed to be a bit nervous, and he noticed her voice was shaking. "Yes, I'm fine. What can I do for you, Henry?"

Jimmy continued to pretend to watch television, but his ears were raptly peeled. He waited patiently for his mother to speak so he could piece things together the best he could. What could his father possibly want with them? He never called or visited since he left with his new girlfriend, and now he just calls out of the blue, talking to Jimmy as if he had just seen him yesterday. It made the boy defensive and uneasy, both for his mother's sake.

"What happened, Henry?" Jimmy turned to his mother to see a concerned look on her face. "Well, there is nothing I can do. What about Mandy? Haven't you called her?"

After another brief moment of silence, Luciana spoke once more. "Like I said, there is nothing I can do. I have a full plate caring for Jimmy, and I cannot afford to have distractions of any kind. To be honest, I cannot believe you have even called me for solutions to your personal problems!" She paused and then put the phone to her chest and turned to her son. "I don't know, Henry. All I can do is ask him." She turned to Jimmy, covering the mouthpiece of the phone as she did. "Do you want to speak to your father?"

Jimmy shook his head vigorously, stuck out his tongue, and turned back to the television. "No, Henry, I'm sorry. He doesn't want to talk right now; he is in the middle of his favorite television program, and I am trying to cook supper. Maybe next time."

They all knew there was very little chance there would be a next time any time soon. Henry O'Brien had burned all of the bridges that led to his ex-wife and small son. Neither had any desire to rebuild them, either.

Luciana hung up the phone and took a deep breath. Jimmy turned to her, worried about her emotional state. She was trying to appear normal, but he could see the stress in her eyes.

"What did he want, Mommy?"

She quickly put a smile on her face. "Oh, it was nothing. Nothing at all, Jimmy. I need to get back to supper."

She headed back to the kitchen, stopping only to run her fingers absent-mindedly through her son's hair, then she was gone. Jimmy followed her with his eyes. He wasn't buying it. His father wanted something, and it made him sick that he had enough guts to bother his mother for it.

He rose off the floor and went into the kitchen, where he stood leaning against the door frame. "Mommy, you said that you and I don't lie to each other."

Luciana had busied herself with turning the chicken thighs over in the frying pan. "It is adult business, Jimmy. It is not for a young boy to worry over such things. Besides, it is not our problem, it is his. There is nothing we can do for him, and even if there were, I would not do it."

Jimmy walked to the table and sat down at his place. "So, if it doesn't matter, what was it?"

Luciana put the spoon on the spoon rest and turned to him. She leaned against the counter and crossed her arms. She began to weigh her words carefully, remembering her son's young age.

"Well, your father has gotten himself into some trouble," she began.

Jimmy waited patiently for her to continue. She looked to be struggling as with what to say, and he was never the type of child to push his mother too fast. Finally, she said, "He has taken something from someone that didn't belong to him, and the police have taken him to jail. Kind of like the club of robbers you told me about from *Men in Blue*."

Jimmy sat up straight; now she had his full attention. "Was he calling you to ask for bail money?"

Luciana looked at her small son with surprise, and she had to work to keep herself from smiling. "How do you know about bail money, young man?"

"From TV, Mommy," he replied simply. "Is that why he called you?"

Luciana nodded and turned back to the stove. "I told him he should call Mandy, but he said she… she ran away."

Jimmy turned this new information over in his mind. None of it surprised him, nor did it upset him in the slightest. A good man, a man like Captain Steele, would never leave a woman and child. But a man who would is the same kind of man who would steal and rob. That was, after all, what he heard his mother saying his father did.

"So he should be in jail if he has been stealing. Don't you think, Mommy? All bad guys need to be in jail, so they don't hurt anyone else. That's what I think anyway."

Luciana stopped stirring the fried potatoes and turned to Jimmy. "Yes, that is exactly what I think too."

Jimmy stood up. "Good then. I'm gonna go watch *ThunderCops*; *Men in Blue* is over now. Okay?"

"Sure," she said. "I'll call you when it's time to eat."

Jimmy smiled at her and went back to the living room. He turned the television to the proper channel, and a rush of color from the cartoon *ThunderCops* filled the screen. He sat on the floor and pretended to pay attention, but his mind was really on Henry Thomas O'Brien.

He did not feel pain over his father; as a matter of fact, he felt as if the crime his father had committed just showed him what kind of person the man was. He would not be like him, no matter what. What he really wanted was to thank him for showing him exactly what and who he did not want to be. Like Captain Steele always said, "We make our own choices, and we choose our own road."

No, Jimmy O'Brien would be nothing like his father. He would use his father's behavior as a map that showed him exactly how to not get lost. Right then and there, sitting in front of his favorite cop cartoon, Jimmy flipped the switch of emotions that pointed to the man that had fathered him. From that day forward, Henry O'Brien would be just another person, another bad guy who hurt others for his own benefit.

Jimmy focused on the television and laughed at the next joke that was made. It wasn't so much funny as distracting. He didn't care at all for Henry O'Brien.

Jimmy and his mother sat at the table eating wonderful fried chicken with Italian seasonings, fried potatoes, and corn. Jimmy was telling her all about the episode of *Men in Blue* that his father had interrupted. Even though he had missed the last ten or fifteen minutes, he did not tell her that. Instead, he simply drew up his memories of the plot and filled her in. She listened eagerly and asked all the right questions, and Jimmy's heart swelled with love.

He was just about to take his last bite of potatoes when the doorbell chimed. "Do you want me to get it, Mommy?"

Luciana shook her head and wiped her mouth with her napkin. "No, darling. You finish up; I'll get the door, then I'll be right back."

Jimmy took his last bite and then took his plate and milk glass to the sink to rinse them off. When he was finished, he walked back into the living room to see his mother seated on the couch with a strange woman. The woman had her back to him, but her voice sounded like she was crying. Luciana had concern all over her face, and she was even holding the woman's hand consolingly.

"I don't know what I will do, but I will never go back," the woman was saying. "I just wanted to tell you how sorry I am for interfering in the lives of you and your son."

Jimmy approached the women slowly, and his mother noticed him almost immediately. She smiled at him, then at the woman. "Miss Foster, I would like you to meet my son Jimmy," she said with pride.

Jimmy walked up to the woman, who finally turned to him. He was smiling, his hand extended to shake hers, but when he saw her face, his smile faltered. She had been beaten or been in an accident, or something. Miss Foster had two black eyes, cuts, and scrapes on both cheeks and her forehead, and a fat lip with a cut down the middle. She smiled timidly, and Jimmy also saw that one of her top front teeth had been broken in two.

It took him a moment, but Jimmy was able to regain his composure and smile at her once again. His mother had taught him to always be polite and to never hurt another's feelings if he could help it. He was sure it would hurt her feelings if he brought attention to her face.

"Hi," he said as he gently shook the woman's hand. "I'm Jimmy."

She gave a small chuckle, even though there were tears in her eyes. "Hi, Jimmy. My name is Mandy Foster. I am… was… a friend of your father."

She took her hand from his and began to root through her purse. After a minute, she produced a tissue and began to wipe her eyes. Jimmy noticed that her blond hair was scraggly and that she had a long tear in the jacket she was wearing.

He knew right away that this was the woman Henry, his father, had left them for. At first, the young boy wanted to be angry, but then he thought about her face and the phone call from his father earlier. Instantly his heart told him what had happened. Even though he was only six, he knew that man had beat this woman up. She was probably even the person he had stolen from. He knew that the truth was she didn't really interfere with his mom and Henry's marriage. No, she had done him and his Mommy a great big favor.

Jimmy turned to his mother. "I'm going to my room to read before I go to sleep. Will you come in and let me know before you go to your job?"

Luciana smiled at him. "Of course, my love." She reached for him, and they hugged briefly, then she planted a kiss on his forehead. "I'll be in before I leave for work."

He turned back to Mandy Foster. "It was nice to meet you, Miss Foster. I hope you have a good night."

"Thank you, Jimmy," she replied. "You too."

With that, he went to his room and shut the door securely behind him. His curiosity wanted to dictate that he ask his mother what had happened to the woman, but even as he put on a t-shirt and shorts and grabbed a book, he knew he would not. If she shared anything with him, that would be fine, but otherwise, he felt he should leave it alone. He lay down on his bed and thought about Henry O'Brien, and the indifference he felt earlier turned to hatred.

Before he opened his book, he got down on his knees next to his bed, just as his mother did every night. He looked up to Heaven and began:

"Dear God, please help Miss Foster. Please heal her

up so she can be pretty again. Maybe someday she can have a good husband, one that treats her nice. Please take care of her the way my Mommy takes care of me, and God, please make sure that Henry has to go away. I don't think he needs a wife or even a girlfriend. I don't know what happened, but you do. Mommy says you always make everything right, so I know you will make this right, too. Thank you, God. Have a good night."

With that, Jimmy climbed in his bed and began to read, waiting for his mother to come in and tell him she was leaving.

R.W.K. Clark

CHAPTER 4

School ended that year with a rush of elementary excitement. All the first graders were already looking forward to second grade in the fall, but before that, they could barely contain themselves regarding the summer break. But Jimmy was as giddy as the rest of the students, he controlled himself, looking forward to the end of the day.

True to his word, Jimmy didn't play with Kevin Marshall for the rest of the year. As a matter of fact, he never played with him again outside of required classroom games and activities. He kept his distance, and he did it for his own good. His Mommy always said bad company corrupted good character, and he understood what that meant.

He did continue to play with Brad, and they even took to a new student who began attending at the beginning of April. At first, they had not taken much notice of him, but after a couple of weeks, Jimmy saw that the other kids were picking on him quite a bit. He invited the boy to play Cops and Robbers with him and Brad one day, and the duo became a trio once again.

His name was David Strickland, and he had moved

to Bernalillo, New Mexico from Texas at the very end of March. He dressed a bit differently than the other kids, which was likely the spark that set the fire for the bullying, but Jimmy and Brad had both lived in Bernalillo their entire lives, and they knew all their classmates. Jimmy, especially, was not afraid to stand up to that kind of behavior.

Kevin Marshall had taken notice of the new friendship the three boys were forming, and though he simply watched from afar, he seethed with anger inside. He wasn't angry at the new kid. After all, how could he be? That kid was just trying to get by. Besides, Kevin had no interest in him whatsoever. He wasn't even angry with Brad, even though Brad wouldn't play with him anymore, either. Kevin knew the reason Brad was distancing himself had everything to do with that brat Jimmy O'Brien, and that was who he hated.

He blamed Jimmy entirely. Jimmy had managed to not only stop being his friend, but he had taken away his other friend as well. The three boys had a bit of a confrontation during the last week of May regarding the issue.

David, Brad, and Jimmy had been out in the field, past the playground. It was the very same field they had played Cops and Robbers in with Kevin, only Kevin wasn't playing anymore. He watched with envy as Jimmy and Brad, obviously the cops, chased David around with their fingers pointed in classic gun-like fashion.

He had meandered in their direction with a scowl on

his face. He had held back his feelings ever since they stopped hanging out with him. He wasn't even positive what the reason was, but he assumed it was because he wanted to be the cop sometimes, and he figured Jimmy didn't like the competition. If Kevin had his way, he would get Jimmy alone someday and kick his butt good.

The three boys didn't take notice of him as he approached, and this irritated him even more. He stopped and watched them as they sat on the ground, pretending to be in cars on a high-speed chase. Finally, he lost his patience.

"Hey, you guys!" he yelled. "I wanna talk to you!"

All three of the boys turned to him immediately. Brad looked a bit intimidated, and David looked confused, but Jimmy stood up immediately and began walking toward him; the other two quickly followed suit, though they trailed behind him. Jimmy looked Kevin in the eye as he neared him, never flinching once.

"Hi, Kevin," he said without a smile. "What's up with you?"

Kevin crossed his arms over his chest and shifted his weight from one foot to the other. "Wondering if I could play with you guys, I guess."

Jimmy turned and looked at both David and Brad; they seemed nervous. Then he turned back to Kevin. "I don't think that's a very good idea," he replied.

Kevin felt his emotions flare. "Why not? What did I ever do?"

The two boys behind Jimmy were silent, but Jimmy had no problem speaking for all three of them. "You know what you did, Kevin."

Kevin was turning it over in his mind, thinking about the last day they played together, and he was genuinely confused. "I don't know what you guys' problem is, but I think you just wanna be the cop all the time. You don't wanna share being the cop, so you got rid of me, huh?"

The new boy David spoke up. "He lets us be the cop with him, so that doesn't make sense."

Kevin turned to David, his eyes flashing. "This ain't even none of your business, kid. You don't have nothing to do with this."

"Fine," Jimmy said with a rough edge to his voice. "You don't talk to him, and he won't talk to you."

"Then I'll say it to him," Brad spoke up. "He lets us be cops, too, so that was a dumb thing to say."

"So what is it then, huh?" Kevin's voice was starting to take on a high-pitched whining quality. "You guys never even told me what I did wrong, and I know I did nothing, not to either one of you guys, ever!"

Jimmy nodded, a determined look on his face. "You're right, Kevin. You never did anything to Brad or me, at least, not that I know of. But for all, we know you might have, and we are just walking around not even knowing it!"

"No, I never! So what was it then?"

Jimmy took a step toward his former playmate. "You steal from people, and we don't want no friends that steal. You can't trust people who steal, even if they call themselves your 'friends.'"

Kevin looked confused for a moment, almost as if he had no idea what they were talking about, but it didn't take long for it to come to him. "That? That money? I didn't take it from you, did I? No! That girl isn't even no friend of yours. What do you care?"

Jimmy shook his head. "No, but if you'd steal from one, you would do it to another. That's just bad, and it makes me sick. We don't want to hang out with no bad people. Not real ones, anyway, and you are a real one."

"You jerk!" Kevin appeared to be full of rage now. His fists were clenched, and his face was red, but he didn't advance toward Jimmy; he only began to yell. "You think you're so cool, but you are just a big loser. Nobody wants to really be on the side of the cops! You just want to look good all the time. For the teachers, for the other kids, everybody. Why you're nothing but a mamma's boy, are you?"

Jimmy just stood there and watched as Kevin put on his show, but he felt terribly angry. Kevin wanted to make him look bad when Kevin was really the bad one. Even right then, at that very second, Kevin was doing nothing but making excuses for being bad and trying to put the attention on Jimmy, but he saw right through it.

"See how you are acting?" Jimmy asked him in a quiet, yet stern voice. "This is why you don't have any friends, Kevin Marshall."

Suddenly, Kevin cried out loud and ran for Jimmy full force. He hit the boy, and both of them flew to the ground, where Kevin then put his weight on top of Jimmy and began to punch him. He got only about three punches in before Jimmy finally defended himself. While Kevin was pulling back to punch him for the fourth time, Jimmy slugged him in the chin, knocking him backward onto his back and making him dizzy. He bit his own lip when he was struck, and blood oozed out of the wound.

Jimmy jumped to his feet and stood over Kevin with his own fists clenched. "You might bully and steal from others, but you aren't gonna do it to me. Do you understand me, Kevin Marshall? You're not gonna do it to me, or to anyone else while I'm around!"

Suddenly Mrs. Edwards had appeared out of nowhere, blowing her whistle and swinging her arms. When she got to the boys, she had let the whistle drop from her mouth, and she grabbed Jimmy by the back of his t-shirt. He didn't put up a fight, and when she realized that he wouldn't, she reached down and pulled a vertigo-stricken Kevin to his feet.

"Boys!" she yelled. "What is going on here? You know it is not okay to fight!"

Kevin immediately began to struggle against the teacher's grasp, Jimmy looked up at her and reply, "Yes, ma'am."

Mrs. Edwards had looked at each one of them, then asked, "Who started this?"

Kevin began to struggle again. "He did! Jimmy did! He's been picking on me for a long time!"

"That's a lie!" It was the voice of Brad Fuller, and he sounded both disgusted and angry. "Mrs. Edwards, we were just playing here, and Kevin came up and started to try and argue about why we wouldn't play with him. Jimmy told him why, and it made him mad, so he tackled him and hit him, three whole times! He's lying!"

By that time, Kevin had lost his breath entirely. He was panting heavily, and his face was bright red. He shot a glare at Brad and then looked back toward the ground.

"Is this true? Kevin?" When the boy didn't respond, Mrs. Edwards said, "Well, all four of you will come with me to Principal Day's office. I'm sure he will get to the bottom of this." With that, she began to march Jimmy and Kevin toward the building while David and Brad followed.

Now here it was, the very last day of school, and all the students were seated in the final assembly listening to Principal Day give the farewell speech. Jimmy sat recalling the events of that day, and it stirred up a bit more anger inside of him. He had not gotten into any trouble due to the truth winning over Kevin's lies, but for the remainder of the year, he had tolerated Kevin's evil looks and shaking fists.

Jimmy was glad the year was over. Next year he would be in second grade, and in no time at all, he would go to junior high. He was patient, and he was very mature for his age. He would see to it he succeeded, no matter what others tried to do to him.

He was determined to be an overcomer, to come out on top. He was determined to be a policeman. That way he could deal with all the Kevins in the world.

He looked over at Brad and smiled. He wondered

what life would be like when they grew up, what kind of grown men they would be. He found himself hoping that Brad was never tempted by the bad people to be a bad person himself.

As usual, Jimmy wanted only what was best for those around him.

∞

"Finally, Jimmy, the last day of first grade. How do you feel?" Luciana had just returned from work to find Jimmy seated at his usual spot in front of the TV. She had gotten things out of the refrigerator for supper, and now she was in the living room talking to him while there was a commercial.

Jimmy smiled up at her proudly. "Good. What's for supper?"

"I thought I would make your favorite tonight. How do hamburgers and fries sound to you?"

His smile grew. "Awesome!"

"Well, you go ahead and watch your show," she said. "By the way, I don't have to work at the laundry tonight, so I thought we might walk up to Cone King and have ice cream after supper."

He nodded enthusiastically, and his mother went into the kitchen. Jimmy looked back at the television for only a moment, though. Today, for the first time in a long time, they played an episode of *Men in Blue* that he had never seen, and it had upset him a bit. It wasn't over, but he wasn't interested in the ending; he would rather talk to his Mommy and hang out with her.

Jimmy stood up and made his way into the kitchen.

He had his toy holster and gun on, and usually, he spun the gun and shot it the whole time he was playing with it, but today it hung limply from his hip. He took a seat at his place at the table and made himself comfortable.

"Mommy, can I hang out in here with you?"

Luciana turned to him, a hamburger patty in her hand. She was concerned right away; his voice had sounded off to her. She searched his face before turning back to the food she was preparing.

"What's the matter, my love?" she asked.

He was quiet for a moment. "Will you tell me again about how you and daddy met? About our life together before... you know... before he left?"

Luciana kept her back to him. "You don't remember the story?"

Jimmy shrugged to himself. "Yeah, I guess, but I need to be reminded."

The truth was that Jimmy had some questions, but he didn't want to just ask them off the cuff. He wanted to hear it again so he could be sure he was asking the right things, because, while his curiosity was about his father, it was also about what he knew his father had become.

"Okay," his mother replied. "Let's see. Well, your daddy... I mean, your father, was born and raised in New York City. Remember I told you about New York, and how very big it is?"

"Yes."

"Well," she continued. "Jimmy mommy and daddy, Grandma and Grandpa O'Brien, were from Ireland, and they came to the United States so they could be free and have good jobs and a good life."

Jimmy spoke up. "Now tell me about you."

Luciana put the second burger in the pan and adjusted the heat on the burner. Then she bent over to get the mini deep fryer out of the lower cupboard. She turned it on to heat up the oil and turned to Jimmy.

"I was born in Portofino," she said with a smile. "Do you remember where Portofino is?"

"Italy," Jimmy replied with a giggle.

"Yes! I came here with my mama and papa to live when I was very, very small." She wiped her hands on a towel. "My mama and papa were your Grandma and Grandpa Marcella. As you know, you have not met them; they have gone to Heaven to be with Jesus."

His mother's parents had been killed in a subway accident in New York City shortly after he and his parents moved to New Mexico. Jimmy did not ask her to tell him that story because it had nothing to do with his reasons for asking her to talk to him about the past, but mostly because it hurt her to do so. He looked at her with patient expectation and waited for her to continue.

She turned around to the sink and began to peel potatoes. "I met your father at my junior high school dance. He did not go to my school; he was older than me and went to high school. But I liked him very much anyway, and he liked me. We began to have dates."

"How did you know he liked you, Mommy?" Jimmy asked.

Luciana smiled and got a faraway look in her eyes, even staring up at the wall from the half-peeled potato in her hands. "He was so sweet, Jimmy. Just so sweet. He looked at me as if I were a princess, and he spoke to me like one, too. He brought me at least one flower every day, sometimes more! He held my hand every time we were together, and sometimes I would catch him staring at me as if… as if I were an angel." She turned and looked at her son shyly. "It would make me blush."

"Your cheeks are red now, Mommy," Jimmy said with a smile.

She waved the potato at him as if to shoo him away. "Anyway, we liked each other very, very much."

"Then what?"

Luciana went back to her peeling. "Well, we dated up until his graduation; I was in the tenth grade then. Henry, I mean, your father, wasn't planning to go to college. See, he had a job waiting here as an account executive with a new computer company. It was for a lot of money, and it was promised to him by his uncle. The future was very, very bright for him."

She rinsed off the peeled potato and picked up another from the sink. "He was to leave to come here to Bernalillo two days after graduation. The week before he took me to supper at a wonderful Italian restaurant, the food tasted just like my mama made! During the meal, he asked me to marry him and come to Bernalillo with him. We would already have a house and a car. His uncle had seen to everything!"

Jimmy turned to her, excitement from the story running through his small brain. "What then?"

"I told him, yes, but he must ask my papa," she said, the smile fading from her face. "You see, mama and papa had plans for me to go to college in New York. I knew it would be a big problem, but I hoped…"

Luciana rinsed off the second potato and then flipped the burgers before peeling the third and last potato in the sink. She started slicing them into fries as she continued. Her face was much more somber now as she spoke.

"The next day, while I was studying, Henry came to the house to speak to Papa, to ask him for my hand in marriage." Luciana continued to slice the potatoes, but this time with a bit more speed and force. "At first, Papa invited him in with a smile. They chatted about baseball; that was Papa's passion, you know. Then, after a moment, Henry told Papa about his new job and all its promise. He told him about preparing to leave for Bernalillo, New Mexico."

She picked up the sliced potatoes and put them in the fryer basket, then gently lowered the basket into the hot oil. After she set the timer, she sat at the table across from Jimmy and continued. She played nervously with the corner of a dishtowel as she spoke.

"At first Papa was excited for him, and even offered him great congratulations. But then your father brought up the subject of marriage." She paused and looked at Jimmy. "Before, when I told you the story, I told you lies, Jimmy. I said we were married in a church, and it was a very happy affair. I am sorry to say this was not true. I will tell you the truth now."

He wanted to ask her why she lied, but he could see by the look on her face that she regretted it. Jimmy decided he would stay quiet and listen. She had apologized, and that was enough for him. He trusted his mother, and if she had lied to him, she had felt like she had a good reason. He nodded at her and smiled his forgiveness. Luciana smiled back and went on with the story.

"He told Papa he loved me very much, and he wished to take care of me forever," she said in a low voice. "Papa politely told him no, so your father asked if he would consider allowing it after my graduation. Again, Papa said no. He told Henry that, not only did he and Mama expect me to attend college, they would only allow me to marry a nice Italian boy, a boy from the Old Country, and one who had gone to college himself."

Luciana's eyes began to water with tears, but she looked up at Jimmy and gave him a smile to reassure him she was okay. She wiped her eyes with the dishtowel and stood to check the fries and hamburgers. "They began to holler at each other loudly; Henry was upset, but Papa was furious. He kicked Henry out and told him never to come back, and while he wished him the best, I would not be allowed to ever see him again."

"What happened, Mommy?" Jimmy asked, a concerned look on his face. "What did Henry do?"

Luciana gave her son a look of surprise at his use of his father's Christian name, but she did not correct him.

She lowered the heat on the burgers and took the fries from the oil, hanging the basket on the side of the fryer. She sat back down and thought for a minute before continuing.

"Well, of course, I heard everything. I was supposed to be studying, but I had been hiding at the top of the staircase listening," Luciana said with a smile. "When I heard your father leave, I thought Papa had ruined my life; I thought I would die from the heartache! I ran to my room and buried my face in my pillow. I stayed there crying until Mama called me for supper. When I went down, I made sure my face was washed, and my eyes were clear. Papa would have taken the strap to me if he thought I had eavesdropped.

"Your father came to my window that night," she continued. "He looked as broken as I felt. It was then that he told me his plan. On the day he was to leave, I was to pack a small bag and meet him at the bus. He would use some of his savings to buy me a ticket, and together we would travel to New Mexico. There was to be a stop in Las Vegas, and there we would get married. Then, there was nothing anyone could do. We would live here in Bernalillo together, in our home. He would take care of me, and we would have a family. We would be together forever."

Luciana reached over and stroked Jimmy's small hand with love. He offered her an affectionate smile in return. "So you did it?" he asked.

She nodded. "That is what we did. Now here you are, and I am happy, even if forever only lasted a very short time. I have you, you see. You are all I want or need."

With a pat on his arm, his mother stood and made their plates. She put extra ketchup on his for his fries, which he loved, then put the plates down and poured the milk before sitting back down herself to eat. The two ate in silence for a few minutes, then Jimmy spoke up.

"Now tell me the rest, Mommy."

Her eyes snapped up right away and began searching his face. He didn't expound on the request, but she knew what he meant. She looked down at her food for a moment, then said, "What do you mean?"

Jimmy put his fork down and looked at her. "After that, Mommy. All the rest of the story, you know, the one you never tell me. How we got here."

"Jimmy, I…" Luciana shook her head. "I don't believe that is a story for children."

He sat back stubbornly, but his tone remained respectful. "I am old enough. I know he is a bad man, probably worse than ever. Please, because I need to know." He paused for a moment. "I know he did that to Miss Foster. Did he ever do that to you?"

She took a deep breath and put her hamburger on her plate. "Okay, Jimmy. I will tell you some, but not all. Not all is for you."

After wiping her mouth, she continued. "To answer your question, no, your father never laid a hand on me; he never hurt me, at least not that way. Everything was fine, at least, it was until you came."

"It was my fault, all the bad?"

Luciana shook her head. "No! It was never your fault. You see, he had big plans, and he spoke the right words, but when the reality of being a man came, he just wasn't ready."

She gazed out the window for a moment before continuing. "You came, and your father loved you, but began to pull away. He took good care of us because he had a good job, but he stayed gone all the time, saying he was 'working.' When he did come home, he slept on the couch, and he became very cruel with his… his words.

"One day he came home and told me he was in love with another, and he was going to live with her. His uncle found out and fired him on the spot; he said he would not have such behavior tarnishing the O'Brien name. Henry didn't care, and he did what he wanted. His uncle gave me enough money to move away and make a new start."

Jimmy was confused. "Why didn't we stay in the house?"

"Because the house was owned by the company, and it was only for the man who would work the position your father was in," she replied. "Besides, I didn't want to stay there."

"It was Miss Foster he left with?"

Luciana nodded. "Yes. He couldn't keep a job after that, and he even had a hard time getting good work because he did not go to college."

The boy's face hardened. "Did he do crimes for

money? Is he a bad guy? Is that why he is in jail?"

She looked at her son fondly. He was so smart! "He did some things that were wrong for money, but I don't know what. I do know that he is in jail for two things. First, he stole from an old couple. He told them he would fix their roof, then took their money and never came back. He did not tell me that, Miss Foster did."

"So, when he came with the money, she asked him where it came from. He didn't want to tell her but finally did, and she called the police. When he found out, he beat her up. So he is in jail for both, and she is leaving and going home to her parents in Nebraska."

Jimmy went silent; it was his turn to do the thinking. He felt rage at the man who was his father, and he hoped he never got out of jail again. He also felt a joy that his father was not in his life. He wanted nothing to do with the man ever again. He also felt pity for Miss Foster, who tried to do the right thing and paid the price for it.

"Jimmy, finish your supper now. It is getting cold," Luciana said softly. "Remember, we are going for ice cream."

He smiled at her and began to eat, though he had no appetite. He cleaned his plate for her sake, and then he helped her clean up by rinsing the dishes. Afterward, they walked, hand in hand, to the Cone King, where Jimmy had a banana split, and his mother had a vanilla cone.

That night, he tossed and turned. He wanted to be a policeman more than anything now, and he hoped that when he was, he would run into Henry O'Brien. Then, and only then, he believes his life would be complete.

CHAPTER 5

Seventh grade

"Alright, everyone, I'll expect a five-page book report from each of you by Friday on *To Kill a Mockingbird*," said Ms. Stout. "Remember, if you want an 'A' it will have to be more than reflective ramblings. I expect you to break down each character, and include either the morality, immorality, or both of each one, as well as how it has been of consequence to them, and why you see them the way you do."

Jimmy scrambled to write down the teacher's instructions as the bell suddenly rang. Students to his right and his left began to bolt for the door, laughing and talking loudly as they departed in chaos. Only he remained seated as he jotted his notes furiously.

"I'm sure you will be one of the A's, Jimmy."

He looked up to see Ms. Stout leaning against her desk and smiling at him. He smiled back and tucked the paper he was writing on into his notebook, then began to gather his things. Finally, he stood with a stack of books in his arms.

"Maybe," he replied, "But not if I don't have the assignment written down right."

Ms. Stout gave him a chuckle and walked to the chalkboard, where she began to erase it. "I wish I had two-hundred more just like you, Jimmy O'Brien."

"See you tomorrow," he said, and he left the room.

The hallway was filled with students tearing through lockers, chatting with friends, and running to get to their next classes. Jimmy had geometry next, and he was going to head straight there. His locker was on the third floor, with all the other seventh graders, and the math lab was on the same as English, so he always took his geometry books to Ms. Stout's class with him to save time.

He walked quickly down the hall and had nearly reached the math lab when he heard his name being called behind him. He turned to see Brad Fuller speed-walking towards him. Jimmy remembered he was supposed to wait for Brad outside of English, and he groaned to himself for forgetting.

"Sorry, Brad," he said as the boy caught up. "I completely forgot."

The two turned into the classroom together. "No problem. I got sidetracked in science anyway. I just wanted to make sure we sat together. Otherwise, we're both gonna have to partner with someone else, and you know how I hate that."

They chose two seats at the same table in the second row of the class right next to each other. Geometry and most other math-based classes were the only classes at Mesa's Edge Junior High where seats were first come first served, and if students had to partner up for any reason, they had to partner up with the person at their table. On numerous occasions, the boys had been forced to partner with others, and it proved to be very uncomfortable for both of them.

Jimmy was not one of the most popular kids in school, and neither was Brad. They were still close friends and had remained such over the years, though David Strickland had ended up working his way into a more popular group. There were many times Jimmy and Brad found themselves either being the punchline to the jokes of their peers or being outright bullied. Neither would ever retaliate; rather, the situations motivated them to focus even harder on who and what they wanted to be.

Brad had decided he wanted to be an attorney, and he buckled down on all his studies to ensure it would be so. Jimmy, of course, was still set on a career as a police officer, and he did the same. He had his entire life's course plotted, and no one would distract him, especially not some slacker with no goals or ambition. Jimmy knew that someday he would be arresting those same people, so he worked hard to keep a social distance.

"Don't forget, we have that special assembly after this class," Brad said. "All regular last period classes are canceled for the seventh and eighth graders."

Jimmy nodded. "Yep. Have you heard what the assembly is for?"

"No," Brad replied with a shake of his head. "All anyone knows is that it's about some special program that is going to be offered to students during the summer break."

Jimmy laughed. "We'll see how many people actually go the extra mile and sign up."

"Attention! Eyes up here, please!" Mr. Gordon, the geometry teacher, was calling the class to order. Everyone looked at him, and the talking slowly died down.

Pencils in hand, Jimmy and Brad gave the man their full attention, as usual.

∞

At 2:42 that afternoon, right after sixth period ended, the two boys sat in the auditorium with all the other seventh and eighth grade students who attended Mesa's Edge Junior High. They were leaning close together and chatting. All the other kids were yelling and hollering, and some were climbing over seats and throwing things. Jimmy and Brad talked about getting together to study, and they waited patiently for the assembly to start.

Suddenly Jimmy felt something strike him in the back of the head. It wasn't painful, but it was enough to jerk his head forward and surprise him. He turned around to see who or what it was, and that was when he saw Kevin Marshall sitting in the seat directly behind him with a scheming smile on his face.

"Well, hey, chump!" Kevin said. "I'm sorry; did I bump your little head?"

Jimmy ignored the boy and turned back to the front of the auditorium. Kevin Marshall had been trying to make his life hell since first grade, and he found that the best way to deal with it was to ignore the boy. As a matter of fact, ninety percent of the bullying Jimmy had endured had been at Kevin's hand, but Jimmy refused to let it bring him down. The kid had even gone so far as to incite others into bullying him. Brad suffered for it as well, but he didn't let it get to him any more than Jimmy did. Both of them knew what Kevin was made of, and they had confidence in themselves, even when it hurt.

"Knock it off, Kevin," Brad said. "Don't you have anything better to do, like study maybe?"

Kevin leaned forward between them so both of them could hear his hissing voice. "How about if after school you both grow some guts and meet me at the edge of the woods by the park. Then I can show both of you who really needs to study, you worthless punks!"

Jimmy and Brad stared straight ahead and ignored him. When he realized that he wasn't getting anywhere with either of them, he simply sat back in his seat, his face covered with a nasty sneer.

Suddenly the talking in the auditorium began to ebb, and the boys noted that Mrs. Joyner, the principal, was on stage. She was holding up her arms for silence. It took her a while, but soon the din died down, and she was able to gain the attention of all the students.

Once the students had gotten control of themselves, she began to speak. "I want to thank all of you in attendance for coming today. This is a special assembly, as you all know, and it is being held to bring attention to a special group. The Junior High Police Academy of New Mexico is an organization whose focus is on bringing students and police together so fear and false impressions can be eliminated. They also provide a summer program to seventh and eighth-grade students who are interested in possibly studying law enforcement in the future."

She gestured to a policeman in full uniform who was standing to her right. "This is Lieutenant Joe Ortega. Lieutenant Ortega is here to tell you about the academy and its purpose and programs. Please give Lieutenant Ortega your full attention, please."

Mrs. Joyner smiled at the man and then took a seat at the rear of the stage. The officer stepped up to the podium and cleared his throat. "Good afternoon, students, and thank you for giving me some of your time today. I am Lieutenant Joe Ortega, and I represent the Junior High Police Academy of New Mexico on a part-time basis. I am also a full-time officer with the Albuquerque Police Department. Today, I would like to share with you some details about the academy, and offer you an opportunity to participate in some of its programs, if you so desire."

Jimmy's heart was pounding, so loudly in fact that it was drowning out every sound except that of the voice of Joe Ortega. To the young middle school student, it seemed that the policeman was speaking only to him, though. He had forgotten the fact that the auditorium was filled with students other than himself. Jimmy knew that the words coming from the man's mouth had been words he had been waiting to hear for as long as he was alive.

He looked to his right, then to his left. Some kids were snickering quietly to each other, others were staring off into space, and yet others were reading books. It seemed to Jimmy that not one student besides himself, including his good friend Brad, was at all excited about the fact that a young police program was being offered in New Mexico.

Lieutenant Ortega continued. "I am not here to take up much of your time; your studies are very important to your future. Rather than rant on about the abundance of benefits that can be derived from participation in this program, or all of the wonderful activities offered, I just want to let those of you who are interested know that you can sign up for participation after this assembly by simply speaking to myself and Principal Joyner. We will take your name, as well as the name and telephone number of your parents or guardian, and we will give you a free packet of information to share with them. Thank you for your time, and have a wonderful day, kids."

That was all it took. The students all but rampaged their way to the auditorium doors, making their escapes as quickly as possible. Jimmy waited patiently for all of them to clear out so he could approach the principal and Lieutenant Ortega, both of whom were now seated at a table on the stage, chatting with each other.

"Are you coming?" Jimmy turned to see Brad looking at him expectantly. Then the young man smiled sheepishly and offered his friend a grin. "You're going up, aren't you man?"

Jimmy smiled back. "You bet I am. Are you heading to class?" He already knew that Brad was going to pass.

Brad nodded and patted him on the shoulder affectionately. "I'll see you after the last bell, okay?"

He stood up and left, and Jimmy stood as well. He maneuvered his way past the few stragglers that were left and made his way to the front of the auditorium at a relaxed pace. He didn't want to seem too eager, but the truth was that he could hardly wait to give them his name and get his hands on that packet. He couldn't wait to share it with his mother.

Jimmy climbed the few wooden stairs leading onstage and approached the two adults. They immediately looked up and grinned at him welcomingly, and he did the same in return. His heart was still pounding, and he was beside himself with excitement. When he reached the desk, he offered Lieutenant Ortega his hand, but before he could speak, Mrs. Joyner began introductions.

"Lieutenant, this is the very young man I told you about," she said. "Jimmy O'Brien." The two shook hands. "I just knew this would be a perfect fit for you, Mr. O'Brien! I am pleased that my prediction was accurate."

"Have a seat, Jimmy," the man said. For the first time, the boy noticed that a chair had been set up across the table from the adults, and he obliged. "Tell me about yourself. How long have you been interested in policing?"

Jimmy looked down at his hands, which were fidgeting nervously in his lap, and he shrugged. "As long as I can remember I have wanted to be on the side of the good guys, sir."

Ortega nodded. "Do you have any concerns?"

"Like what?"

"I don't know," the man continued. "Anything at all that you feel may hold you up or hold you back?"

Jimmy quickly nodded his head. "No, sir. I mean, I work very hard to keep my grades up. I also focus on not allowing negative people or distractions into my life." He paused for a moment.

"What is it, O'Brien? What are you concerned about?"

Oh, how he loved to be called by his last name by a cop! His stomach fluttered as if it were full of butterflies. He hesitated for only a moment longer, then looked Ortega in the eyes. All Jimmy saw was honest interest coming from a man that simply reeked of integrity. He held back no longer.

"What if... what if I'm too small?"

Jimmy was a skinny boy, and shorter than the other kids his age. The things that he had which made up for it were determination, intelligence, and gumption. But those three things had never been enough to rid him of the nagging feeling that he would never quite measure up.

Ortega didn't miss a beat. With a serious look on his face he said, "Young man, I have full confidence that by the time you are ready to enter the academy, you will be plenty big enough. It's common to be a bit smaller at this age, son. Why, when I was your age, I was the smallest in my class."

A surprised look came over the boy's face. He looked at the man sitting at the table; he was nothing but muscle and bulk. When he had stood next to Mrs. Joyner on stage, he had towered over the woman, and she was known for being somewhat of an Amazon, as the other kids liked to refer to her.

"Really?"

Ortega smiled. "Absolutely, O'Brien. You bet. Now, how about you give me the name of your parents and a number I can reach them at. Then, take this packet home and share it with them; see what they think." He reached across the table and handed Jimmy a plastic bag with the state of New Mexico on it and the motto 'New Mexico Junior Police Academy: Building a Safe Tomorrow for All Through Our Students.'

He took the bag in his hands as if it were gold and set it gently on his lap. "It's just my mother and me," he replied. "Her name is Luciana, and she is amazing. She will be very excited for me about this opportunity." Jimmy rattled off the number and stood. He held the bag safely in one hand and held out the other to shake once more. "Thank you so much for considering me, and I look forward to your call to my mother, sir."

The man stood and shook Jimmy's hand while Mrs. Joyner filled out a pass for him to return to class. She handed it to the boy and said, "Jimmy, I am so pleased you are interested. I just knew you would be."

"Thank you both," he replied, then turned around and headed off the stage and out of the auditorium.

Mrs. Joyner turned to Lieutenant Ortega. "I apologize that the kids didn't show more interest." She stood to move the table and chairs to the rear of the stage. Ortega began to assist her.

"No, please don't apologize, ma'am," he said. "We would rather have one child, boy or girl, as interested and as passionate as O'Brien, than all of them just trying to get out of class or wasting our time. Wouldn't you agree?"

While the two adults were talking and cleaning up, Jimmy was closing his packet safely into his locker, his face and eyes beaming with pride and joy. He was so surprised about the program, and he was beside himself with excitement. Mother would be too.

It had turned out to be an extraordinary day.

R.W.K. Clark

CHAPTER 6

Jimmy finished out the day at school as best as he could, but he found it to be a bit of a struggle. All he could think about was Lieutenant Ortega and the Junior Police Academy program. He couldn't wait to tell his mother, but of course, she wouldn't be home for a bit. By the time he got back to their apartment and let himself in, all he could do was watch the clock and wait while half-watching an episode of *Detective Suspense*. The program had been out for the last five years, and it was based on real-life cases. He loved it.

He put some potato chips in a bowl, coupled them with a glass of milk, and sat before the television. Jimmy tried to focus on the program, but his ears were peeled listening for his mother, so he was nearly lost on the plot after only fifteen minutes in. As he munched on his chips, his eyes shifted to the plastic bag marked with the New Mexico Junior Police Academy logo which contained the packet. He had purposefully not looked at it yet; he wanted to share it with his mom, but he was just about to lose his resolve.

Finally, he heard shuffling outside the front door. Jimmy jumped up and quickly opened the door to see his mother juggling grocery bags. Without a second thought, he took the bags and headed for the kitchen.

"I thought you would never get here, Mom," he said. "Now I know why it took you so long. How was your day?"

Luciana sighed. "Long, but over now. I don't have to work at the laundry tonight. I traded a shift with Thelma Rogers. I need a rest, that's for sure."

Jimmy put the bags on the counter and began to unpack them while she put her purse and jacket in the closet. "How about you, Jimmy. How has your day been today?"

He picked up the pace, a smile plastered to his face. "I'm glad you asked. My class had a special assembly today, and I have some things I want to show you."

Luciana plopped down on a chair at the table and ran her hand through her hair. "Thank you for your help, son," she said as Jimmy put the grocery bags into their designated spot. "I'm ready when you are."

He bolted into the living room and grabbed the bag, then returned to the kitchen. Luciana saw that her son's eyes were alight and he was beside himself. Seeing him so happy and excited brought a smile of pride to her face and a powerful rush of love to her heart.

"Okay," he began. "So, our assembly today was only for seventh and eighth graders. It was a short presentation made by a policeman named Lieutenant Ortega, and he talked just a little bit about a program called New Mexico Junior Police Academy." He held up the bag so she could see the logo.

Luciana read the words on the bag and asked, "Junior Police Academy? What is this?"

Now Jimmy began to unpack the bag quickly. "I don't know very much myself, Mom. I wanted to wait to go over this information with you together. I was the only student who showed interest, though. Oh, and the policeman has your number. He will be calling you to talk about it also."

From the bag, Jimmy brought out a stack of colorful booklets and some official-looking forms. He put the forms aside and took the booklets in his hand. He wanted to sit closer to his mother, so he pulled his chair beside her so they could both see them at once.

The top booklet featured the smiling face of a young man about the same age as Jimmy. Next to him was an officer in full uniform with his hand on the boy's shoulder. The Junior Police Academy logo was across the top; the bottom sported the words: 'Who We Are, What We Do.'

Both of them sat there just looking at the booklet. Luciana glanced at her son and saw that he was just sitting there, a goofy smile on his face, staring at the cover. She almost had to put her hand over her mouth to stop herself from bursting out in laughter.

She gave him another minute, then said, "So, Jimmy, are you going to read it to me?"

"Oh, yeah!" He jumped a bit, then composed himself and opened the cover. Then Jimmy began to read.

The program brought students and officers together

to bridge the gap between the law and misinformed children. It was effective in teaching interested youngsters regarding what the purpose of the police truly is, and it seemed to build a great level of much-needed respect between the two. Officers would work with the kids to teach them leadership, community contribution, and school safety, not to mention mentoring and minor training for those interested in a career in law enforcement.

With that booklet out of the way, Jimmy moved on to the next. This one explained the history of the program, and it also introduced the professionals who were involved. It told a bit about each person and even had a picture of them individually next to their biography. Finally, it introduced the members of the Junior Police Academy board and talked briefly about how these people organized the needed elements of the program itself.

The next pamphlet was the one Jimmy was truly interested in. It was a narrow white booklet on shiny paper, and the cover read "Training Courses at New Mexico JPA." The boy's hands were almost shaking as he proceeded.

"The first course is called Getting to Know Each Other," he began. "The Getting to Know Each Other course has been implemented to allow students to become more familiar with who law enforcement really is, and what their true mission is in society. By taking the time to do this, false perspectives are eliminated, and students are better able to understand the truth about police and the laws they enforce on a day to day basis." He paused, but only for a moment, then he continued to read through the rest of the section.

The next course was entitled 'Police Officers of the USA.' From what both Jimmy and his mother read, the purpose of it was to begin to work on character building skills by being exposed to a variety of officers and their individual positions, and by the demonstration of integrity by each. The students would actually spend time with police from detectives to special agents, and from patrol officers to SWAT members and bomb squad specialists. It was more than Jimmy ever could have dreamed of!

Finally, there was a section called 'My First Day.' Cadets would hear, in detail, from each of the officers listed. They would talk about themselves and give details about their jobs and why they do them. The pamphlet discussed why this day was the most important day in the entire program, and from what Jimmy read, he couldn't agree more.

There were only two booklets left. One focused on the JPA's and how to get a hold of anyone at the Academy to discuss participation, and it detailed the included application forms. The last booklet gave details about a leadership group which met weekly for support, education, and assistance for the students who participated. When Jimmy was finished going over all the information, he took a deep breath and sat back in his chair, a dreamy, distant look on his face.

Luciana knew that he was beside himself with awe

and pleasure, and she did not want to interrupt him. She stood and began to prepare a single cup of instant coffee for herself, giving him time to daydream. As she stood at the stove waiting for her hot water to boil, the telephone rang.

Jimmy snapped out of his reverie. "I'll get it," he said, and he began to get to his feet, but his mother stopped him.

"No, Jimmy," she said, patting him on the shoulder. "You take some time; I'll get it."

As his mother made her way to the phone, Jimmy stood and went to the bathroom. He closed the door behind him, but there was no need to lock it. He didn't go into the bathroom to use it, he went in to think, and he didn't want to be distracted by the phone call.

Jimmy flipped on the light and looked in the mirror. It was written all over his face: he was ecstatic! The New Mexico Junior Police Academy was one of the best things to come into his life that he could remember. It was the perfect opportunity to get exactly where he wanted to be: on the police force, stopping crime and making a difference in the world that mattered.

He looked at his reflection for only a moment longer, then he left the bathroom and went into his room. He wanted to write in his journal and record the way he felt at that exact moment. He wanted to write about all of it, so he could look back when he had made it and see how much had changed in his life. Jimmy plopped down on his bed and took his spiral notebook out from under his pillow. It was one of several, all of which were cherished possessions.

He took his pen from his nightstand and began to write furiously.

R.W.K. Clark

CHAPTER 7

"Henry James O'Brien!"

Jimmy stood from the chair he was seated in and began to cross the platform, walking toward Chief Harold Barnstrom, the administrator of the Academy. Applause broke out once again as he approached the man to accept his Certificate of Completion for the Junior Police Academy. Jimmy glanced out into the audience and saw his mother clapping furiously; he could even see the tears of pride in her eyes from where he stood.

He reached the man and held out his hand for the handshake, his other hand prepared to take his certificate. Flashes went off around him, and as instructed, he turned to the audience and held up the certificate, giving an opportunity for much-desired photos. His shoulders were squared with pride, and his smile was dazzling.

The New Mexico Junior Police Academy had turned out to be far more fulfilling than Jimmy ever could have imagined. He learned so much he could hardly contain the knowledge, and he met men and women who demonstrated a level of integrity that Jimmy didn't know really existed in the world. He finally felt as if he had a much clearer vision of his desired path that he ever had before, and he was deeply satisfied with the experience.

He left the stage and took a seat next to it. There were a total of fifteen students who had attended the Academy with him, and there were still five who needed to be given their certificates. Afterward, there would be a banquet with family and friends. Jimmy was starving, and he could smell the waiting meal, which made his stomach rumble loudly.

He looked to his right to the audience. His mother was waving at him madly, and Jimmy waved back. He couldn't believe how blessed he was to have her for a mother. The evening he shared the program information with her was the very evening Lieutenant Ortega had called. Jimmy had written in his journal, then fell asleep with his face on his notebook. When he woke the next morning, his mother was at the table filling out his application paperwork for the program, and she had supported him abundantly all the way through.

The only person he was missing was Brad Fuller. He wished Brad could have come to the ceremony, but his friend was away at summer camp. Little did Jimmy know that he and Brad would grow further and further apart. Not due to Brad going down a wrong path, rather he would simply begin to make another group of friends, and Jimmy's focus would remain steadfast and sure. Not even his friendship with Brad would be able to deter him from his goals.

For the time being, he pushed his friend out of his mind. He put his focus back on the ceremony and continued to watch all of the other kids get their certificates. He was proud to be a part of the program, and he offered hearty applause for each of his fellow students.

Finally, the last student, the only female in the class, received her certificate. Chief Barnstrom waited for the applause, and the flashes, to die down. It was then he was able to address the crowd.

"As you know, all of you are welcome to attend the banquet, if you are able," he said. "Thank you for your support in allowing your young man or woman to attend the academy. It means the world to us, and it means the world to the future of this country."

There was another round of applause as the crowd began to stand and gather their belongings. Jimmy made his way to his mother through all the people. After scanning people as he walked, he finally spotted her. She was clutching her purse and wrap and talking to a police officer in full uniform. Jimmy didn't recognize him, but he was too excited to give it much thought.

When Luciana spotted him, a broad grin spread over her face. She nearly dropped her things trying to open her arms for a hug, which Jimmy welcomed warmly. They embraced for a moment, then his mother put her arm around him and held him to the side to introduce him to the officer she was speaking to.

"Jimmy," she began, "This is the chief of our own

police force in Bernalillo. Chief Matias Garcia, this is my wonderful Jimmy."

Chief Garcia was beaming as he shook Jimmy's hand with gusto. "Great job, young man. I have heard quite a bit about you, you know."

"Yes, sir," Jimmy replied. "I hope it has all been good."

Garcia chuckled and smiled at the young man. "All of it! Say, would you mind if I joined you and your mom for the meal?"

Jimmy returned the officer's grin and nodded. "That would be great."

The three made their way into the academy's large gymnasium, but on that evening it resembled anything but. Music was playing, and large, round paper lanterns were hanging from the ceiling. Long tables with white tablecloths sported candles and other decorations, as well as place settings meant to dazzle. On the far end of the room, a line of servers were lined up waiting for the actual meal to begin. Otherwise, Academy graduates and their guests, as well as an abundance of police, all milled around talking, smiling, and laughing.

"So, where do we sit?" Luciana asked, trying to conceal the excitement in her voice.

Jimmy took his mother by the arm. "We were instructed to choose our own seats, for both ourselves and our guests. Where would you like to sit, Mom?"

Luciana shrugged. "Close to the door, I think. That way I can find the ladies' room easily if I need to."

The three chose seats at the end of the table closest

to the exit. Jimmy and his mother sat down, but Garcia remained standing to push in Luciana's chair. Jimmy took notice of the action, and it made him smile. He never would have thought of it, and it was a great example to him of how to behave when in the company of a lady.

"Can I get you something to drink?" Garcia asked the pair.

Luciana looked up at the man. "Ice water will be fine for me, thank you."

"Jimmy?"

"Oh, I can get the drinks if you prefer," he replied.

Garcia patted his shoulder. "Naw. You and your mother need a moment alone together. What would you like?"

"How about a soda?"

"Soda it is." Garcia disappeared into the crowd.

Jimmy turned to his mother. "Pretty nice event, huh Mom?"

Luciana was beaming. "I have never been to anything nicer in years. I am so proud of you, Jimmy. Now, to finish high school, attend college, and then off to the police academy for grown-ups."

"That is the plan, for sure."

She took her son by the hand, and the two of them watched the people mingle all around them in silence. Before long Matias Garcia reappeared with three beverages in his large hands. He placed them before Luciana and Jimmy, then had a seat across from the boy with his own beverage, another soda.

"Jimmy, your mother tells me you have wanted to be a police officer your entire life."

Once more a smile covered the boy's face. "I cannot remember a time I didn't want to be."

Garcia took a long drink off his soda and continued. "Me too. As soon as I could walk and talk, I was playing Cops and Robbers."

His response made Jimmy laugh. "In elementary school, whenever I went out to recess, I played that with my two closest friends. Well, until second grade, anyway."

"What happened in second grade?" Garcia asked.

Jimmy shrugged. "Well, one of my friends got in trouble for stealing from a classmate. He was the one that always seemed to have an attitude about everything. When he stole from that girl, I decided I didn't have room in my life for someone like that."

Garcia nodded at him. "Good decision. Are you two friends now?"

Jimmy looked away and glanced around the busy gymnasium. "No. If anything he sort of picks on me, but I don't care. I'm not going to let that kind of behavior distract me."

Matias looked at Luciana, whose gaze was glued to her son. Her eyes were shining with pride that was almost tangible, and the policeman found himself reminded of his own mother. It made him happy.

"So, do you play any sports in school, Jimmy?" Garcia took another drink of soda as he waited for an answer.

Now the young man squirmed a bit in his chair. "Not really. I'm on the small side, you know. I guess I just figured I would give my all to my studies."

Matias Garcia smiled and nodded as his own boyhood flashed through his mind. "I can understand. The police academy has a pretty tough physical program, so that is something you may want to keep in mind. But really, the most important reason for participating in athletics as a teen is to learn teamwork, drive, and organization."

He met the boy's gaze and saw that Jimmy was paying very rapt attention to what he was saying. "Are there any sports that capture your interest at all?"

Jimmy thought about it for a minute. "I like baseball, I guess."

"Perfect!" Matias replied. "I would encourage you to participate at school, and even try to get involved with a local summer team, maybe through your church or Bernalillo's recreation department. You will be amazed at how much personal growth you can experience through athletics."

Jimmy smiled and nodded at the man. "I understand. I will begin to look into it right away, sir. I believe that's very good advice."

The lights in the gym came up a bit, and Chief Barnstrom announced the serving of the food. Graduates and guests began to take their seats, and the servers started the job of taking plates of green salad to the diners. When Jimmy, Luciana, and Matias had theirs, the officer made a suggestion.

"I hope you don't mind, but I am going to say grace over my food," he said. "Would you two care to join me?"

Even out of the corner of his eye, Jimmy could see the rush of pleasure that came over his mother's face at the man's suggestion. Jimmy himself thought it was incredible that a big, tough cop prayed. He was astounded and impressed.

He felt like he was right where he belonged in his life.

∞

Luciana O'Brien didn't drive, and she and Jimmy had planned to take the bus back home from the academy. When Chief Garcia became aware of that fact, he insisted on driving them. Even though Jimmy's mom was usually too prideful to accept such an offer, she actually seemed relieved this time.

Jimmy sat in the back seat reliving his evening while the two adults chatted in the front seat of the large Pontiac sedan Matias drove. When they got to the O'Brien's apartment, Matias walked them up, and while Luciana unlocked the door, the officer spoke briefly to Jimmy.

"So, how do you feel about coming to my gym with me sometime?" Matias asked him. "You may be surprised what you will learn, and how much you will like it."

The boy could not believe his luck or conceal his excitement. "You bet! I mean, yes sir!"

"Well, I go three or four times a week," he said.

"How about I get your number and give you a call. We can go in the evening to fit your schedule if that would work for you."

Jimmy vigorously shook Matias' hand. "Perfect." The officer jotted the number and promised to call before saying his goodbyes and leaving.

It could not have been a more perfect night for Jimmy O'Brien. He didn't think he would be able to sleep, so he wrote all about it in his journal. He didn't want to forget a moment of it.

He woke the next morning once again asleep on the notebook, with spiral wire marks on his face.

CHAPTER 8

"Okay, boys, great practice. Now hit the showers, then go home and hit the books. See you tomorrow for more of the same." Coach Mick Ryan gave the baseball team a brief wave before taking his clipboard and heading off the field.

Once he was inside, Jimmy tossed his glove into the assigned bin and headed for the locker area. As he prepared to shower, he thought about how much had changed in his life in the last few years since leaving the Junior Police Academy, and all of the thoughts made him smile.

He let the hot water run over his head as he soaped up. He had to go straight from the high school to his part-time job at Harver's Grocery to bag. He had taken the job the summer after ninth grade, and for the first two years, worked only in the summer because his mother wouldn't allow him to let work interfere with his grades. Now he was a junior in high school, and his mother had allowed him to work up to twenty hours a week. It made him happy to be able to contribute to household finances.

As Jimmy dried off and dressed, he listened to the

voices of his other teammates. Some of them talked about their girls while others ribbed their best friends or slapped their rear ends with a towel. Laughter echoed through the locker area, and it brought Jimmy a touch of melancholy. He wished Brad Fuller had opted for baseball instead of football.

But the fact was that Brad had filled out quite nicely in the last year-and-a-half, while Jimmy was still a bit slight. Brad had gone out for football in the ninth grade, and now it was one of the main things he focused on. The pair still hung out sometimes between classes or on the weekends if one or both of them didn't have to work, but their time together had reduced greatly. It was the normal process of things, but Jimmy missed his friend often, nonetheless.

He hiked up his jeans, leaving them open to tuck his button-down shirt into. Next, Jimmy put the shirt on and began to fasten the buttons. The locker room was growing fairly quiet, and Jimmy knew he needed to pick up his pace if he didn't want to be late for work.

He was just tucking his shirt into his jeans when he heard the voices. They came from the next row of lockers over, and even though Jimmy couldn't identify the voices, he could make out the words.

"So, did you like that last stuff, man?"

The sentence stopped Jimmy dead in his tracks. He froze and peeled his ears to listen closer. His heart was pounding; something inside of him knew exactly what was being discussed from that first sentence.

"I did, I did. Can't wait to try this out," another

voice replied. "You said it's better, right?"

"Yep, but it'll cost a bit more."

Jimmy quickly fastened his button-flies and began to creep to the end of his locker row in his stockinged feet. When he got to the end, he stopped and continued to listen. He didn't want to miss anything.

"Here's forty bucks." Jimmy heard the ruffle of paper. "Thanks, man. See you this weekend at the bonfire?"

"Sure thing. See you at Buck's"

The voices were getting further away. Jimmy went around to the row the voices had been coming from just in time to see the locker room door swing shut. A frail-looking young man with thick black-framed glasses sat on a bench at the end of the row. He was trying to take a broken lace from a sneaker.

"Was that you talking over here?" Jimmy asked him.

The kid jumped, startled by Jimmy's presence. "Nope. Wasn't me. It was one of the baseball guys."

"Who was he talking to?" Jimmy asked. "I mean, the voice sounded familiar. I think it was an old friend of mine." The lie dripped easily from his lips.

"I don't know. It was some kid in a leather jacket."

Jimmy nodded. "Thanks."

He headed back to his locker, his mind racing. Someone on his team was taking drugs? He couldn't be sure, but he was willing to bet that was exactly what the two boys were talking about. He wished he would have had the nerve to confront them, but he was just now starting to shake all of the bullyings he had endured through junior high and high school. He was ashamed of the fact that he still seemed a little gun shy.

Once he had his shoes on, Jimmy grabbed his backpack and headed out of the locker area, taking time only to glance at the clock on the wall above Coach Ryan's office window. It was nearly 5:45 and he had to be to work for a 6-10 shift. He needed to move and was more relieved than ever that Harver's was only five blocks from the high school.

For the entirety of his shift, Jimmy thought about the conversation he overheard in the locker room. It had his guts in knots, and all he could think about was talking to his friend and mentor, Chief Matias Garcia. He and Garcia had become very close; in fact, the man and Luciana O'Brien had become a bit more than friends. Jimmy almost looked at Matias as the father he never had.

It seemed like eight hours instead of four before Jimmy was able to clock out and head home. He all but jogged the distance; he wanted to talk to Matias, but he also had some chemistry homework and an essay to finish. He was anxious to get there and take care of everything so he could get a decent night's sleep.

When he got home, his mother was already asleep. During the rest of his walk, he had rethought going directly to Matias with the drug issue; he wanted to have some kind of proof. Otherwise, both he and the chief would end up looking very foolish indeed. Jimmy thought he would talk to Luciana, but upon seeing her peacefully sleeping, he put the idea directly out of his head.

Grabbing a snack, he went into his room to finish up his homework. Jimmy found it difficult to concentrate, and because of that, it took him until nearly two in the morning to finally wrap it up. When he was finished, he turned off his light and, after turning his alarm on, lay on his bed on top of his blankets. Finally, he wouldn't have to fight the thoughts of the conversation he overheard in the locker room.

If only the boys had been speaking just a bit more loudly, then perhaps he could have recognized one or both of their voices. The boy who had been in the row of lockers with them had played dumb, but Jimmy was sure the kid knew who they were. He was probably scared to death of the consequences of 'snitching' them off. Jimmy knew that the boy was a victim of bullying, just as he was. Bernalillo High was a small school; whether you knew someone by name or not, everyone knew everybody. Or, at least, they knew about them.

Jimmy was just about to doze off when a thought hit him and jerked him from his light sleep. Yes, he would approach the boy once more and try to get him to give up what he knew, but he would also take his mini-cassette recorder. He would put a new tape in it and hide it on top of the lockers right before practice. Hopefully, he would capture the drug dealer on tape by simply recording. But would the one tape be enough? He wouldn't be able to flip it over. No, he would need two recorders.

His mother had one just like his. Both of them were

gifts from her boss at the laundry when she had still been employed there. He had given one to Jimmy for study purposes, and one to Luciana, though she had never used it. In the morning, Jimmy would ask her where it was, and if he could use it.

With a plan formed, Jimmy was finally able to doze off. His rest would be short, and it would also prove to be restless. He dreamed of being on a high-speed chase, pursuing a teenaged drug dealer who was hurting kids with his wares. So real was the dream that Jimmy jerked and mumbled as he slept.

He would certainly feel his exhaustion the next day.

"Mom, I was wondering if you still had that small tape recorder that Mr. Peterson from the laundry gave you. You know, the one like mine." Jimmy and his mother sat at the breakfast table the next morning, enjoying each other's company and some steaming hot coffee.

Luciana got a look of confusion on her face initially, then her eyes lit up. "Yes! I had all but forgotten about that little gadget. Do you need it for something?"

Jimmy nodded and drained his coffee cup before standing to pour another. "I do. I want to conduct an experiment at school, and I will need to record."

"What about yours?" she asked.

Jimmy shrugged and sat back down. "I have it, and it's fine. It's just that the project will require the use of two recorders."

Luciana stood and left the room. Within only a few minutes she returned, toting the tiny device in her small hand. "I think the batteries inside have gone bad."

Jimmy took it from her and pushed a couple of buttons. It didn't work, and so he removed the batteries and threw them in the garbage. "I have a brand new package; I'll replace them. Do you mind if I use it?"

"Of course not," she replied as she bent over and planted a kiss on his head. "The tape inside is new as well; I have never used that thing."

He gulped down the cup of coffee quickly and stood up. Jimmy put the cup in the sink and then stretched out before saying, "Well, I better be going. I was up pretty late studying."

"You look tired." Luciana had a concerned look of love on her face. "I wish you wouldn't pack your schedule so full, Henry James."

Jimmy smiled at the beautiful woman, then stooped to kiss her cheek. "I picked up one of Mike Harper's shifts a couple of weekends ago. He's filling for me, so I don't work at Harver's tonight, mom. Just practice, then home, okay?"

She looked relieved. "Good, good. I will make homemade pizza. Doesn't that sound delicious?"

"Always." Jimmy grabbed his backpack from one of the empty chairs at the table and slung it over his arm. "I should be home by six. See you then. I love you, mama."

Before he walked out the door, he went to his room and grabbed a package of double 'A' batteries and two brand new mini cassettes from his desk. He shoved them into his bag, then headed out, shouting goodbye to his mother once again. He planned to tell his last period teacher that he had to duck out of class a little early for an appointment. Then, he would head directly to the locker room and set up the recorders. In the meantime, however, he was going to be keeping a close eye out for the boy in the black-framed glasses. He knew that if he could just get him alone for a few minutes, he could get him to talk.

The day dragged by. Jimmy couldn't get his little plan out of his mind, and it was much more distracting than he would have liked. So preoccupied was he that he missed the homework assignments in two classes, forcing him to approach his teachers and ask for them to repeat them. It was unlike him, and in both cases the teachers showed concern, telling him he looked tired, and asking if he was okay. He managed to convince them both using only a smile and a bit of humor.

As he was heading in the direction of his last class, Jimmy saw the young man from the locker room. He was at his locker fumbling with the lock while two bulky boys with long greasy hair and fuzz on their upper lips were razzing him. One of them had a cigarette tucked behind his ear, and the other wore a denim jacket with the sleeves cut off; it was covered in motorcycle patches.

"Come on, Lawrence," Cigarette Boy was saying. "All you have to do is kick down with the five bucks, and we'll leave you alone."

Patch Boy chuckled. "Yeah, we'll leave ya alone… until tomorrow!"

Both boys roared with laughter, then Patch tried to knock the kid's binder from his arms. The boy juggled it as he fought to keep it in his grasp. Jimmy was enraged. His anger erased any apprehension he might have felt; all he could do was intervene. Fury took control.

"What the heck is wrong with you guys?" He spit it out with acid on his tongue, almost hissing as he spoke. Jimmy put his arm around Lawrence and turned him so he, too, was facing the two punks. "Don't you have anything better to do than entertain yourselves by picking on this kid? Like, I don't know, bring up your grades, or study, or something?"

Cigarette Boy sneered at him. "Why don't you mind your own business, asshole?"

Jimmy couldn't help but spew a hearty laugh. "Asshole? That's funny. It appears to me that the only assholes here are you two." Now he turned in the direction of the hallway monitor, who happened to be Coach Ryan right then. "Hey! Coach Ryan!"

Patch Boy reached out immediately and grabbed Jimmy by the arm. "Hey! What's your problem, man? We were only talking to Larry for a second before class. No reason to flip out."

Jimmy hissed, glaring at the lying boy. "You were trying to muscle him into giving you his money. I saw you, I heard you, and you're nothing more than a scourge to everyone here. Why don't you beat it, before I get Ryan over here to drag your butts to the office?"

Patch shot a glance at Cigarette, who looked mad enough to crap fire. Jimmy showed no intimidation; in fact, right at that moment, every scene of bullying from his own life flooded his mind full force. He wasn't sure he would be able to get the coach; he would rather pound these losers into the ground with his bare hands.

Cigarette looked at Larry and smirked. "You ain't even worth it," he said. "You better hope we don't get you alone anytime soon, creep."

"You won't," Jimmy assured him. "As a matter of fact, he'll be hanging out with me. If you'd like, we can hook up after school, creep."

Cigarette slapped his sidekick on the arm. "C'mon, Jay. These punks aren't even worth it." The two boys flipped their middle fingers at Jimmy and walked off, their strides cocky and their noses in the air.

Larry breathed an audible sigh of relief, almost doubling over. "Are you okay?" Jimmy asked him.

He nodded and stood upright, then proceeded to grab a book from his locker before slamming the door and locking it back up. "Never ends. It just never ends."

"Well, it ends today, man," Jimmy replied as he patted his shoulder. "What class are you headed for?"

Larry pushed his glasses up. "Civics."

"Come on. I'll walk you." Jimmy knew that walking with the kid would make him late, but he also knew his own personal priorities. Stopping the bullies and dealers was more important. Besides, he was never late. He wouldn't mind detention or extra homework, but he doubted his teacher would give him either.

They began to walk up the hall together, heading for the stairs to the third floor. Jimmy's class was on second, but he would go to third with Larry first. He wanted to talk to him, to put the boy at ease.

"Didn't I see you in the locker room yesterday?"

Larry walked with his head down, making eye contact with no one. "I don't know; I guess."

"Are you on a team?" Jimmy watched the kid closely, but his posture remained consistent.

Larry shrugged. "No. Coach Ryan lets me work out after school. I'm trying to, you know, bulk up." He gave a nervous laugh, and Jimmy noticed he was blushing.

"Good for you!" Jimmy replied. "By the way, I'm Jimmy O'Brien. You are?"

"Larry," he said after clearing his throat. "Larry Tower."

Jimmy stopped and pulled Larry to the side of the hall. "Listen, Larry. I want to talk to you about those boys in the locker room yesterday."

Suddenly the kid began to shift around and fidget nervously. "B-B-Boys?"

"Yeah, Larry. Those boys who were in the row with you." He paused and studied the young man. "If you really want to stop all the bullying, you have to stand up to the bad guys. I've been bullied. I've had enough; haven't you?"

Another long sigh. "Yes."

Jimmy looked around and noticed that the hallway was nearly completely clear. He took Larry by the arm and pulled him into the boys' room. Then he checked under the stalls before turning back to him.

"Together we can make sure those kids, both in the

hall and the lockers, never bug you again, but you have to help me."

Panic filled the boy's eyes. "I... I..."

Jimmy calmed his voice and softened his eyes. "Look at me, Larry."

The boy slowly forced himself to look up.

"The boys from the locker are doing drugs, Larry. And it's the drugs that make them the jerk they are. They need help."

Larry shifted from one foot to the other. "I don't know..."

"Larry," Jimmy continued in a low voice. "It's the kids like us, the good kids that have to stand up to the bad ones. Or, the truth is, they will never stop."

Now Larry glanced briefly at his wristwatch, then he thought for a moment. "Okay, look. I'll tell you the only information I know, but then you have to keep your eye on me. I'm not saying we need to hang out or even be friends, but if either of them gets in trouble, it's gonna come back on me."

"Nothing is going to happen to you, Larry," Jimmy swore solemnly. "I promise with my life."

Larry thought for a moment longer, then looked around the bathroom once more before saying in a whisper, "The one who was buying the drugs was named Dean. That's all I know."

"What kind of drugs?"

Larry shrugged with frustration. "I didn't see them. They were in the other boy's fist, hidden. Look, I'm already late for class; the bell is going to ring any second."

With that, Larry Tower darted toward the door. After he opened it, he turned back to Jimmy. "I hope nothing happens to me. It's not like you can really protect me. I know that."

Larry left the bathroom just as the bell pealed obnoxiously, its warning echoing through the halls. Jimmy barely heard it though. He leaned back against one of the sinks, his mind racing.

Dean. There was only one student named Dean that played baseball and would be in the locker room at that time of day. Sure, Jimmy supposed it could be another Dean rather than his teammate. Maybe it was another student who was there to work out, like Larry Tower.

No, he thought. Larry was an exception. Jimmy knew Coach Ryan; he was trying to help and encourage the boy. Jimmy also knew with certainty that it had to be the Dean that played with him on the team. It could be no one else. His name was Dean Cormer, and he was considered one of the best athletes at Bernalillo High.

Jimmy headed out of the bathroom and made his way to his final class. He knew which locker was Dean's, and that was where he would be planting the recorders. Instead of sitting through his final period, Jimmy decided he would apologize for being late, take his consequence, and tell the teacher that he had to leave to see the doctor for a check-up. He hated lying, but there was no other way.

As he approached the classroom door, he straightened his shoulders and took a breath. He felt no nervousness, only excitement. He was going to make sure the drug dealing scum got eliminated from the halls and classes of his school. With that, Jimmy turned the knob and entered the classroom.

CHAPTER 9

Jimmy O'Brien lay uncomfortably in a fetal position, the smell of mildew filling his nostrils. He was curled up in a towel bin at the end of the locker row where the boys had done the drug deal the day before. He was covered with wet towels from earlier classes, and they were soaking through his clothes, wetting his skin.

He had begged out of last period, pleading a doctor's appointment. To his surprise, his teacher didn't even mention the fact that he was late to class as well. Jimmy was asked if everything was okay, given his homework assignment, and dismissed. It had taken all of three minutes. He was relieved that there was only one boy from his baseball team in that class, and that kid had been busy gabbing to his neighbor while Jimmy spoke with the teacher.

Next, he had gone to the gym and visited Coach Ryan. He pulled the man aside and gave him the same story, agreeing to make up for the practice with drills, or whatever the man required. He assured Jimmy they would figure something out, but to go on to his appointment. Jimmy had told him he had something to get out of his locker first, then he left the gym and went to the locker room. Once he was there, he got the recorders ready with new batteries and tapes. He made sure they worked, then planted both of them: one atop each row of lockers flanking the bench area between. He wasn't going to miss anything that may happen.

Now he was lying beneath the wet towels, waiting for the practice to be over. He had hidden quietly in the shower area at first, looking at his watch only once, and at that time, he had already been there two hours. His instinct told him another hour had nearly passed; he figured it would be 5:30 soon, meaning practice would be over and the boys would be rushing into the lockers. At 5:20, he had emerged from the showers and turned on the recorders, then buried himself in the towels. Now here he was, waiting.

For the millionth time that day, he thought about drugs being in his school, and the thought made him ill. So many lives ruined by drugs, so many! No, he didn't have any sort of first-hand experience that was true. But Jimmy O'Brien watched TV, and he was a loyal watcher of the news, as well. He knew the impact illegal substances had on lives and the people who lived them, and he hated it.

He carefully turned his head to look at his watch, pushing the light button with his right hand as he did. 5:28. Practice would be reaching an end very soon now.

Just as the thought left his head, Jimmy heard the sounds of boys laughing and yelling. They were approaching quickly, and his heart began to pound with both fear and anticipation. Lord, he hoped something would happen today, but he also knew there was a good chance it would not. If that was the case he wasn't sure *how* he would handle it; he just knew he *would* handle it.

For the next twenty-minutes, boys yelled, and showers ran. It felt like an eternity to Jimmy before he began to feel the impact of wet towels being thrown on top of him like so many unwanted rags, but he was relieved. Finally, they were beginning to leave.

Sure enough, the locker room began to grow quieter as kids filed out and headed for home. Jimmy lay still, waiting for either silence or the last of the kids to talk. He didn't know what else to do.

Just when he thought he was all alone in the area and was nearly ready to leap free of the wet mess which entangled him, he heard the voices. He could tell they were only feet from him, and with no metal lockers between himself and them, he could hear them fairly well.

"Hey, I thought you were good until the bonfire," the first voice said. "How did you go through that already?"

The voice was very familiar to Jimmy, but he pushed it out of his mind for the time being. He needed to focus on the entire conversation. He couldn't let his mind wander.

"I ended up using it to get my homework done," another boy replied in an unfamiliar voice. "It kept me up all night. I'm tired, and I'm supposed to go with my mother to help get ready for a church garage sale this weekend. I'm worn out and beat up, man. I just want another fifty dollars-worth."

The first boy laughed, and immediately Jimmy froze. His heart almost froze up as the realization hit him: oh, he knew that laugh. He knew it all too well. Anger began to course through his veins, and he had to struggle to reset his focus.

When the kid was done laughing, his voice got more serious. "You have the fifty, right? I'm not gonna front it to you, man. I have to re-up tonight, so I need the money."

"Yeah, right here." Jimmy could hear paper shuffling once again.

"Alrighty, then," the first boy said. "I should be good again by tomorrow if you decide you want more. You had better get some sleep tonight, man. I don't need you screwing up; it'll bring attention to me, and I can't have that."

Jimmy could hear their conversation continue, but they were getting further and further from him. After another minute, he heard the door to the locker room slam shut, and the area was completely still. He lay only another couple of minutes, just to be sure he was alone, before sitting up and flinging the heavy wet towels off of his soaked body.

He jumped from the towel bin, shivering as the air conditioning hit his skin. He made a beeline for the recorders, which were still running. He stopped them both, then went to his own locker and got his backpack from it before jogging out of the locker room, his heart pounding. Oh, yes, he knew the voice of the boy who was selling the drugs. As a matter of fact, he knew it all too well.

It was his old childhood playmate. It was the boy who had been pushing him around and bullying him since second grade. It was the boy with no morals, who stole from girls.

It was Kevin Marshall.

∞

"Jimmy, it's good to see you, son. Come on in!" Chief Matias Garcia stood in the doorway of his office at the Bernalillo Police Department. A smile covered his face, and his eyes glowed with pleasure as he gestured for Jimmy to enter and visit with him.

He held the door open for the young man, then closed it securely once Jimmy was inside. Jimmy automatically sat; their relationship had progressed past silly formalities years ago. Inside the Chief's office, Jimmy felt safe and secure. He had been a mess all the way to the station, watching over his shoulder the entire way.

Matias sat in his own seat at his desk and leaned forward on his elbows. "To what do I owe this pleasure? You know, your mom invited me for homemade pizza tonight. Now we can head to your place together."

Jimmy nodded and smiled at the chief. "I need to talk to you about something important, Mat."

The boy's smile did nothing to put the seasoned officer at ease. The smile quickly faded from his face, and he suddenly became very serious. "What's going on,

Jim? Are you okay?"

Jimmy nodded. "Yes, yes. It's not me, I'm fine. Something is going on at my school, though."

"Okay," the chief replied as he sat back in his chair. "What's up?"

The boy began to talk, and once the words started, they could not be stopped. He began by telling him about the initial conversation he overheard in the locker area, then he related his mini-undercover operation to Mat. By the time he was finished, the cop may as well had steam coming from his ears; he had looked both concerned and a bit angry.

"Do you have any idea how dangerous what you have done really is, young man?" His voice was stern, but his eyes were soft.

Jimmy nodded. "Yes, sir. But someone had to do it. This had to be done. What would you do if I had come to you first? Send in an undercover officer from here? To a high school? No, it wouldn't have worked. It would have been a dilemma." Jimmy paused as he dug the two recorders from his bag. "Dangerous or not, now it is done, and I know who the dealer is. I know his voice. I have known him my whole life."

Matias' gaze shifted to the recorders, and a slight smile covered his face. "So, you got them on tape." He looked up at Jimmy again, his eyes dancing. This time his voice had softened. "Did you really hide in wet towels?"

"I did."

Mat stood and walked around his desk, finally

resting his rump on it in front of Jimmy. "Let's hear what you've got."

The two listened to the tape three times. In the end, Jimmy said, "Both tapes are the same; I did two to make sure I got them."

He took the tapes from the recorders and handed them to Mat before putting the recorders safely back into his bag.

"So, who is it, Jimmy?"

Jimmy dropped the bag to the floor and looked up at the chief. Finally, he cleared his throat and said, "Kevin. Kevin Marshall."

Mat smiled and shook his head, more out of sadness and disgust than anything. He stood up from the edge of his desk and walked back to his chair, placing the tapes on the blotter before him as he sat down. "Kevin Marshall. I'm not at all surprised, you know. I guess I always knew he would progress from graffiti and curfew violations. I just never thought he would deal drugs."

Jimmy remained still as the chief spoke, and when he went silent and began to think, Jimmy waited patiently. He was fully aware that Kevin would not be arrested right away; he would have to be caught red-handed dealing drugs. There would have to be a process, some kind of set up, and Jimmy had no idea what the chief had in mind or how he would deal with it.

"The tape said he was 're-upping' tonight, right?" Matias asked.

Jimmy nodded and remained quiet.

Mat nodded. "Well, the only way we can put a stop to this is to either catch him with drugs, which is a charge of possession or to catch him actually selling them, which is a bit bigger. Either way, he will have to do some time in juvenile detention. That should cool his heels, though. Maybe it will even set him on a straight path." The man paused once more, then continued. "You don't know who the other kid is?"

"I think I do," Jimmy said. "The kid that I told you was in the locker area yesterday, Larry Tower, told me one of them was a kid named Dean. There is one Dean on our team: Dean Cormer. I know that Dean isn't the dealer because I recognize Kevin's voice clearly. The dealer is Kevin, so the kid has to be Dean Cormer."

Mat nodded again. "Well, we could always try to bust the Cormer kid with the dope he bought, but first we need to make sure there is no way he is some other 'Dean.' I'll call Coach Ryan at home; we go to the same church. He will be able to tell me if there is more than one kid named Dean in the lockers at that time."

Matias picked up a phone book and flipped through it. He stopped on a page and ran his index finger down it, finally stopping at a name. Next, he picked up the phone receiver and punched numbers in quickly. Jimmy could hear the faint ringing coming from the receiver.

"Mick! How are you?" Matias said. "This is Mat Garcia from the church. How's the family?"

The two men exchanged small talk for a brief moment before Matias finally got to the point. "Listen, Mick. I called for a reason. We have a small investigation going on, and I think you have a kid on your team we may need to talk to. Is there a Dean Cormer on the team?"

Mat listened for a second, then said, "Would there be any other boys by the name of Dean who would be using the locker room at that time, by chance?"

Jimmy could hear the coach's mumbled voice just enough to make out the word 'no.' Matias nodded at the phone and said, "Well, I'm going to have to pay Mr. Cormer a visit. If you see him before me, please don't mention this conversation, will you? It could foul things up for the investigation."

More words came from the coach, then Mat said. "Thanks for all your help, Mick. Give my regards to Trish and the kids. See you Sunday, alright?"

Finally, he hung up the phone. "Okay, it sounds like Dean and his mother were going to be going to church. I'm going to pay a visit to his home and see if I can either talk to him there or find out what church he is at. Looks like you will be having pizza without me tonight, son."

Jimmy sat up straight in his chair, his eyes widening with confusion. "Aren't you going to take me with you?"

"Now Jimmy, you know I can't," the chief said. He saw the boy's eyes fall and quickly tried to rectify the situation. "I'll tell you what, though. You go on home. Have a good meal with your mom; I'll call her and let her know I can't make it right away. I will call you and fill you in as soon as I know anything, alright?"

Jimmy nodded at his mentor and offered him a half-hearted smile as he stood. He grabbed his backpack and slung it over his shoulder, then said, "I sure hope you can stop Kevin. Dean sounded all messed up. I think it's cocaine he is selling, and I can't stand the thought. How many other kids is he selling it to?"

Mat only nodded. "I know, son. I know. I'll be in touch."

∞

For the remainder of the week, Jimmy waited on the edge of his seat for any kind of communication from Matias. He attended school and went to work, but he was always waiting and wondering. At home, he would find himself staring at the phone endlessly, his foot tapping and his mind racing. The only consolation he was able to take was in the fact that Dean Cormer was absent for the last two days of school that week. He knew it was because of the situation at hand.

On Friday, Jimmy did everything the way he always did: he went to school, attended practice, and got in four hours at Harver's Grocery. At practice, there had been a bit of whispering amongst the other guys, but none of it was discernable to him. Unable to grab onto any real answers, Jimmy simply bided his time and waited to hear from the chief.

On Saturday, while sitting at the kitchen table having breakfast with his mother, Jimmy finally got the call he had been waiting so anxiously for. The phone rang, and just as he had done with every ring for the past couple of days, he jumped to his feet and raced for the phone.

He had filled Luciana in on the situation, so she wisely sat back and let him do what he had to do.

"Hello?"

It was Matias. "Hi, Jimmy. How are you, son?"

Jimmy let out a breath. "I'm good. I thought I would never hear from you. What's up, Mat?"

"Well, like I said, it's a process, and that process must be carefully followed to be successful," he replied. "I would rather discuss it in person. I haven't talked to either you or your mother in a few days. Can I come over?"

Jimmy couldn't have been more ecstatic. "Sure! Hold on." He turned to his mother. "Can Mat stop by? He wants to talk."

Luciana nodded and smiled. "See you in a bit then, okay?"

"Sure thing, Jimmy."

The boy could hardly finish the rest of his breakfast as he waited anxiously for Chief Garcia. His mind contemplated and wondered: what had taken place? Had Dean Cormer been caught with the drugs and arrested? Had he led them to Kevin? Jimmy tried to recall if he had seen Kevin at school either Thursday or Friday, but he could not.

After only ten minutes, Matias was at the door, and soon the two were at the table talking while Luciana prepared eggs for the man.

"So, I guess you are wondering what's going on, eh, young man?" Matias began.

Jimmy laughed. "You think?"

"Well," the man continued. "On Wednesday I went with another officer to the Cormer residence. Dean was not at home, as we expected, but I was able to have a long conversation with his father, and I explained to him exactly what was going on. At first, he wouldn't listen, but when I told him about the recordings, he buckled."

Matias had Jimmy's full attention. "What did he say? What did he do?"

"I asked if he had a problem with me searching Dean's room," Mat replied. "I told him that if we found nothing, we would walk away and we would pursue the issue no further. He agreed, my man and I gave the room a search."

Now Jimmy was literally beside himself. "Did you find anything?"

Mat gave a sad sigh and nodded. "Unfortunately, we did."

Rather than responding, Jimmy waited on the officer sitting before him. After about thirty seconds, he sat back and looked Jimmy in the eye. "We found a cigar box. Inside were razor blades, short bits of plastic straws, a small compact mirror, and empty baggies with residue in them."

The boy still waited. He knew that what the officers had found was enough, and he didn't want to appear too eager to see a fellow student and human being go down. He simply searched Matias' face with his eyes.

"We also found a baggie with white powder in it," the chief said. "We tested all the baggies with our field kit, and they were all positive for cocaine."

Now Jimmy sat back and crossed his arms over his chest. He felt anger and relief at the same time. What had happened next, though? Had they been able to get their hands on Kevin Marshall, or had Dean Cormer kept his mouth shut and taken all the trouble?

As if reading his mind Matias said, "We found out what church the boy was at and arrested him there. He spent Wednesday night in juvie, and on Thursday we met with him, with his attorney present. We explained how much trouble he was in, and fortunately, his lawyer was able to convince him to help us out."

Luciana suddenly appeared at Matias' shoulder and put a plate in front of him with fried eggs, bacon, toast, and potatoes on it. He immediately picked up his knife and fork and began eating. The man took a couple of healthy bites and reveled in the flavors before he went on.

"He agreed to attempt to buy more cocaine from his dealer, who he readily confirmed is one Kevin Marshall," he said.

Now confusion came over Jimmy. How was that going to work?

"Matias, he has been out of school for two days! Isn't Kevin going to be suspicious?"

The chief chewed his bite and swallowed it, following it with a large drink of cold milk. "As soon as he agreed to cooperate, while he was still in detention, we had him call Kevin and tell him he was sick. He told him he would likely be out of school for a couple of days but would need to hook up before the bonfire at Buck's place. Kevin bought the story hook, line, and sinker."

Jimmy sat back hard in his chair, satisfied. Yes, something was indeed going to happen to stop Kevin from continuing his rampage of destruction on the students with his drugs. He felt satisfied, and he couldn't be more pleased.

"So what happens next?" he asked.

Mat wiped his mouth with a napkin. "What happens next is, at one today, Dean will call Kevin to arrange a meeting. He will ask to buy one hundred dollars worth of coke, and then he will take his father's car, which he usually drives, to meet the boy."

"When he meets him, they will make the deal, and once Dean is in the car with the stuff, he will head home. We will be watching the whole thing, and Kevin will be arrested immediately." Matias turned to his food and began eating calmly once again.

Now it was time for Jimmy to truly process what was going to happen. Yes, Kevin Marshall was dealing drugs, and not just any drug, but terribly dangerous cocaine. Dean had been caught with the substance, and he was going to assist Bernalillo police in setting up the dealer. Kevin was going to go away. Not forever, but he would definitely do a bit of time, and he wouldn't like it one bit.

Matias finished his breakfast and wiped his mouth one last time before turning to both Jimmy and Luciana. "Thank you. It was delicious. Now, if you will excuse me, I have to get to the station. There is a meeting to put all the enforcing officers on the same page, and then we are heading to the Cormer residence." He reached out and tousled Jimmy's hair. "When this is all said and done, you are going to be something of a hero, son."

He walked Matias to the door and told him to be safe. The Chief promised to fill him in on everything once again, and then he left. When Jimmy returned to the kitchen, his mother was sitting quietly with a somber look on her face.

"What's wrong, Mom?"

Luciana was fiddling with her fingers and staring at them intently. "I am proud of you, Jimmy. You have done the right thing, and it will improve life at your school for you and the other students. But how dangerous will it really be when you are a man and having to deal with these people face to face?"

Jimmy stood behind her and wrapped his arms around her, hugging her tightly. "I will be fine, Mom. Always have faith that good will always conquer and that God is watching over me."

His mother hugged him back, but he knew she was not appeased. He would always be careful, for her sake, but no matter how dangerous things got, he would not give up his dream. He would work hard for the rest of his life to be one of the mighty boys in blue.

∞

Everything went according to plan in the set-up and arrest of high school student Kevin Marshall.

Dean Cormer made the call, and afterward, he drove

and met Kevin at Ironsides Park. There, the young man purchased one hundred dollars worth of cocaine, then he jumped into his father's Explorer and made his way home. Once he got there, the drugs were confiscated by police, and the wire the boy had been wearing was carefully removed. As a result of his cooperation, Dean Cormer faced no charges; the only thing he had to face were his classmates. His family decided it was too much, and eventually, they relocated to Arizona to give the boy a fresh start.

Kevin Marshall, on the other hand, found himself in a world of trouble. Not only was he busted for the sale he made to the Cormer boy, but he was also found to have a full two ounces of the white powder stimulant on his person. He ended up being sentenced to the correctional center for boys in New Mexico until his eighteenth birthday. After that, he would be on probation until he was twenty-one years of age. He overheard at the police station, that Henry James O'Brien, the boy he had considered his arch-nemesis since grade school had played a vital role in his capture and conviction.

Kevin vowed with great conviction to his family and friends that the day would come when he would have full revenge on his former elementary playmate, and he meant it.

Jimmy, on the other hand, was lauded a hero by classmates, parents, and teachers alike. Everywhere he went, he heard about how brave he was and how much he was appreciated. While the attention was nice, it also bothered him a bit; he wasn't trying to gain attention, he was trying to rid the streets and his school of one bad person.

Chief Matias Garcia, as well as Luciana O'Brien, couldn't be more proud of the young man. In the eyes of his mother, Jimmy was nearly perfect. Chief Garcia simply glowed whenever he and Jimmy were together, and if they spoke with other people, he would brag on how far the boy had gone to do the right thing, even putting himself and his own safety at risk. He swore to Jimmy that once he had finished both college and the police academy, he would have a guaranteed place on the Bernalillo force. In Matias' eyes, Jimmy was as close to a son as a young man could get, and he promised to have his back for the rest of his life.

The incident was a game changer for Jimmy O'Brien's life and future career, but no one could fully grasp exactly how much of the game it would come to change.

R.W.K. Clark

CHAPTER 10

Officer Jimmy O'Brien pulled the collar of his rain slicker tightly around his neck. Making sure he had a firm grip on his hot Styrofoam cup of coffee, he took a look out the glass door of the gas station at the torrential rains pouring down. He took a single deep breath, and with his head lowered slightly, he pushed open the door and ran out into the night, trying to get to his squad car as quickly as possible.

Once inside the warm, dry vehicle, Jimmy made sure the doors were locked. Placing his coffee in the cup holder, he proceeded to remove his wet slicker and lay it on the passenger side floor. It wouldn't do to get all of his paperwork wet, and besides, he never did mind a little bit of dirt. Being the only officer working that car he didn't have much to worry about, though.

Finally, he was able to take a breath and enjoy his coffee. He took a short sip, testing the temperature, and then a longer gulp. The coffee warmed him to his toes with a pleasant tingle. Living in New Mexico was a sure way to avoid freezing, but the rain would definitely give one a chill, especially when they were so used to the warm, dry weather.

The police radio was silent except for a bit of static and the sporadic officer check-in or silly one-liner exchanged between officers and dispatch. It was a slow night in Bernalillo. Not that it was always this way; in recent years, the crime rate had picked up considerably, and the cops always had something to tend to.

Jimmy leaned his head back on the headrest and closed his eyes. At twenty-six, he was pleased to say he was exactly where he hoped he would be: a working police officer. Actually, it was better than he had hoped; he was in his hometown, not some huge city with a killer around every corner. No, Bernalillo was the perfect place to police, and he couldn't have been happier.

He had been on the force five years now, and that meant he had fifteen more to go before retirement. It seemed like an eternity, but he knew it would pass all too quickly. When he thought back over his life, he saw clearly that it had passed like a flash, and he assumed that the years to come would do the same. It wasn't so bad, anyway. He was still keeping his eye on becoming chief someday, but he was biding his time. Working under Matias Garcia was a dream come true, so he certainly couldn't complain.

The only thing missing from his life was a woman. He worked most of the time, so he didn't indulge in going out or finding a hook-up. His mother was the only girl in his life at the present time, and he was okay with that. For now, anyway. Jimmy did, indeed, look forward to the day he would meet the one meant for him, and together they would begin to build a family and a life.

For the millionth time, he considered the past, and how he got where he was at that moment...

After Kevin Marshall's arrest, Jimmy had become something of a celebrity with law enforcement, as well as with all the residents of Bernalillo. Sure, he had a couple of dates after that, the most memorable being his prom date, Melody Chapman. Oh, she had been so cute then. One of his long-time crushes. Long, soft blonde hair, accented by light blue eyes. High cheekbones and pouty lips really set off her face. She had been tiny and slight, and he had adored her, but he never shared his feelings with the girl. His focus was on college and the academy, and he was afraid she would be a distraction. Besides, she ended up leaving for UCLA after graduation, and the last Jimmy had heard she lived in Los Angeles and did social work. He put her out of his mind, silently wished her the best, and went on with his life.

After he graduated from the University of New Mexico in Albuquerque, he had earned his criminal justice degree and managed to maintain a four-point average. Being successful in college had consumed his thoughts and his time, but it had been worth it. From there he attended the Albuquerque Police Academy for one year, and once again he finished at the top. Matias Garcia had attended his graduation, in the company of his mother, and when all was complete, he was welcomed into the Bernalillo department with open arms and hearts.

Now, of course, it had been just over five years since all of that had ended. Jimmy lived here in Bernalillo; he had bought a small house during his third year on the force. It was a cute two-bedroom bungalow with a large porch and porch swing. The front yard had a couple nice little flower beds (which he didn't have time to enjoy), and the backyard was fenced in with a chain-link fence, allowing him to have a dog. His furry pal was a black Labrador named Max, and he hung out with him every chance he got. The dog was, after all, his best friend.

He had made many other friends as well. All of them were police officers or worked closely with them. Some of them were the spouses of cops, but just like on television, cops were all family. It seemed no one understood them quite like they understood each other, and they gravitated toward one another naturally, whether intentional or not.

Regardless of the number of friends he had, there was one that he was closest to. Officer Kenny Clark started on the Bernalillo force about six weeks after he did. He took the place of an officer who had been shot down in a gas station robbery on the outskirts of town. The two hit it off right away. Like Jimmy, Kenny had wanted to be a cop for as long as he could remember. He had let nothing steal his vision, and his dream also came true. Unlike Jimmy, he had been raised with his father in his life, but both of his parents had been drug addicts, and that was the catalyst for Kenny's career decision. He let it drive him forward rather than discourage him. The two of them were very much alike in many, many ways.

As for carving himself a niche, Jimmy had managed to do that in spades. He had made countless arrests; some of them minor, a good handful of them major. Even though he was not yet a detective, he had made four good-sized drug busts which managed to rid the town of some very undesirable types, and he had earned recognition each time.

∞

The last big bust he was responsible for was the arrest of a twenty-two-year-old punk from Arizona. He had come to Bernalillo to stay with an aunt under the guise of 'getting on his feet.' Instead, he managed to do a series of home burglaries that had townspeople losing sleep at night. He got away with ten burglaries in a row, and then he attempted an eleventh. A newly installed alarm went off on the house, and by the time he got out and broke into a run, Jimmy and another officer were there. Jimmy gave chase, but he didn't catch the guy.

The next day, while getting coffee at his usual spot, Jimmy noticed a young man wearing a hooded sweatshirt that was identical, at least to Jimmy, to the one the burglar had been wearing the night before. He tried to make eye contact and smile at the guy, but the guy's eyes were shifty, and he avoided looking at Jimmy at all. While he couldn't be positive about the sweatshirt due to the darkness the night before, Jimmy thought it would be appropriate to question the kid. After all, he didn't recognize him as a local; who knew? He noticed that the kid wrote a check to pay for the soda, chips, and cigarettes he was buying, then he left the store on foot.

"Do you know that kid?" Jimmy asked Martha, the cashier at the In-and-Out gas station.

Martha had shrugged. "Naw, Jim, he's new here. I know he lives with his aunt because she always gives him blank checks to use here. She even made it a point to come in and let us know it was okay for him to do so."

"Who's his aunt?"

Martha stamped the back of the check and got ready to put it in the drawer, but stopped. "You know her," she said as she flipped the check over to be sure. "Yeah. Beatrice Thompson, over on Steadway Drive."

She held the check out to Jimmy, and he scanned it briefly. "Thanks, Martha. Never seen him before; I was just curious."

"No problem, Jim. Be safe." With that, she went back to her work.

Jimmy was with a partner that day because it was a Saturday. On the weekends, they usually doubled up in preparation for the partying that would potentially take place. His partner on the weekends was usually Chris Kingston, and that was who it was that day as well. Jimmy climbed into the car and turned to the man.

"Bea Thompson has her nephew living with her. Did you know that? Do you know the kid?" he asked.

Chris had shrugged. "Nope. I don't recall ever

hearing about him."

Jimmy had taken a long pull off his coffee. "Well, he was just in the store, and I think he might have been the one I chased last night on that burglary call. I want to go to Bea's and ask him a few questions."

"Got it," Chris replied. He didn't hesitate; he pulled the squad out of the parking space and headed out of the lot in the direction of Bea Thompson's place, which was only a few blocks away.

They hadn't seen the kid on the short drive, and when they got to the house, all looked quiet. Both Jimmy and Chris went to the door, though Jimmy was the one to knock; he would be confronting the kid and asking the questions. After all, he had gotten the better look at the burglar.

The door was answered right away by Bea Thompson. She was a small, slender lady of about fifty. She had dark hair with a bit of silver in it, and she was dressed in comfortable stretch slacks and a matching smock. When she saw Jimmy and Chris, she gave them a beaming smile.

"Hi, boys! Long time no see, Jimmy!" She had moved to Bernalillo around twenty years ago, and she went to the church Jimmy was raised in.

"How are you, Mrs. Thompson?" he asked. He remembered that she was a widow and that her husband had died when Jimmy was in junior high. She certainly must have been lonely, and he was sure she was relieved to have her nephew with her.

"I'm fine," she answered as she stood back to give

them room to enter. "Come in, come in! To what do I owe this pleasure, boys? Certainly, it's not my sparkling personality!"

Jimmy smiled at her. "Well, that's part of it. Actually, I came to talk to you about your nephew. I heard he was living here with you."

The smile faded quickly from her face, and it looked as though she weren't surprised at all. "Matthew? Yes, he is. Can we step into the kitchen, boys?"

Jimmy nodded, and they both followed her to the kitchen area. There was a small table with four chairs there, and Bea beckoned for them to sit. "Can I get you boys some coffee and cookies?"

Jimmy dropped her surname. "No, Bea. We're fine, thanks."

"Then what do you want to know about Matthew?" she asked as she took a seat as well.

Jimmy cleared his throat. "Well, I saw him a little bit ago at the 'In and Out,' and, well, I'd hate to say this, but he matches the description of a burglary suspect." Bea's entire body stiffened, and her mouth turned into a thin, straight line. "Now, I'm not saying it is him," Jimmy continued in a reassuring tone. "I just want to rule him out if we can."

Bea let out a long breath and sat back in her chair, rolling her eyes with disgust. "Matthew's mother is my sister. She and his father have been horrible parents to Matthew; drugs, bad crowd, and the like. Matthew has been in trouble in Arizona."

"What kind of trouble, Bea?" Chris asked.

Bea began to fiddle with her hands, and her gaze dropped as if to study what she was doing. "Well, he was caught with marijuana a couple of times, and then he was arrested for robbing a house. They tried to charge him with several robberies, but they couldn't prove any of them. The charges were dropped, and he moved here. He said he wanted to start over, to get a job and get on his feet." She paused and looked up at the men, then, lowering her voice she said, "He hasn't even put in so much as an application. I can't get him to do anything. He won't even come out of his room."

Jimmy gave the woman an understanding nod, and he waited a moment before continuing. Finally, he asked, "Is he here right now?"

Tears had begun to form in Bea's eyes. She didn't answer him, she only nodded, then she stood and left the kitchen.

Jimmy and Chris stood up and made their way to the living room. They kept quiet so they could hear what was being said. At first, they heard Bea knock; there was low music playing on the other side of the door. After the second knock, Matthew's voice said, "Yeah?"

"Matthew, would you come out for a minute? I need you to reach me down some light bulbs from over the fridge." Jimmy looked at Chris; she knew he wouldn't willingly talk to them, and she had lied to get him out there. She was suspicious, and if she was, they had good reason to be as well.

The bedroom door opened and Bea let the young man out so he could walk in front of her up the hall.

She closed the bedroom door, and then followed him. When he entered the living room and saw Jimmy and Chris, he completely froze up.

After a couple of seconds, his face turned red. "What the hell is this, Aunt Beatrice?"

"They want to ask you a couple of questions, Matthew." Her voice was like stone, and she had crossed her arms over her chest to let her nephew know she meant business.

The kid looked at them with steely eyes. "Yeah?"

Jimmy started. "Matthew, where were you last night around 8:15?" He took note of the large, gray sweatshirt on the guy; the offender had worn a large, gray sweatshirt with the hood up. On the back were the words "Cop Killa" in black. Jimmy had seen the words clearly during the chase; in fact, they had made him nervous.

"I was right here," came the flippant response.

Jimmy turned to Bea. "Was he here, Bea?"

"I can't say, Jimmy," she replied. "I was at the neighbor's, playing Canasta."

The men turned their eyes back on Matthew. "Well?"

"I was here," he repeated, his voice deepening with anger.

Jimmy nodded. "Okay," he said. "Will you turn around please, Matthew?"

"Why?"

"I need to see the back of your shirt so I can rule you out," he replied.

Matthew didn't move; he simply stared Jimmy in the eye, and Jimmy could see the wheels turning in his head. Suddenly the boy darted to the left for the hallway, pushing Beatrice to the floor. She hit it with a thud and cried out.

Jimmy saw it though: the back of his sweatshirt said 'Cop Killa.'

The two officers darted down the hall after him, and when they got to the door, they saw Matthew sprawled out on his bed. He was aiming a handgun directly at them, his face red and his eyes crazy.

"Go away!" he screamed. "If you go away, I will too. You won't have to worry about me again."

Jimmy held his hands up to show he wasn't armed, and just as he opened his mouth to speak Matthew jerked the gun, and it went off in a deafening explosion. Jimmy didn't take the time to look around. He pulled his own gun and planted a bullet in the young man's left thigh, causing him to drop the gun and cry out loudly in pain.

∞

Jimmy O'Brien jerked himself out of his deep thoughts. He looked around, his hands shaking and his breathing rapid. His heart was beating so hard he could hear it. He had remembered so clearly that he had completely lost track of the here and now.

He was in his squad car, still parked at the In and Out. The rain had let up, but it was still coming down. The radio was crackling loudly, breaking the silence and making him jump. He reached out and turned down the volume before calming his breath and getting control of himself.

Chris Kingston had died that day, right in the doorway of Matthew Freeman's bedroom. Jimmy had administered CPR, but the bullet had hit him directly in the heart; the cop hadn't stood a chance. Jimmy had and still did, feel responsible.

But, regardless of the death of the officer, he was called a hero once again. He was a hero because he stopped the serial burglar who was threatening the town. The kid went to prison, and people could sleep well at night.

Everyone but Jimmy that is.

Chris wasn't the first officer to die in the line of duty that he knew. There had been a few, which was a few too many. Chris was the only one he had been with at the time of death, and because of that, he would always be distraught and heartbroken. He would always feel responsible, because he would never, ever forget.

He took a long drink of his coffee, draining the cup dry, then he shook his head violently in an attempt to make the thoughts go away. The radio crackled again:

"Domestic call at 322 Marlon St. Apt. 4," it said. "Nearest squad please respond."

Relieved, Jimmy grabbed the mike. "I've got it. En Route to 322 Marlon."

He hung the mike up and pulled out of his spot, his mind on the task at hand. If anything put him back to being himself, it was doing his job. Dispatch couldn't have timed it better. Jimmy O'Brien was relieved.

CHAPTER 11

Luciana O'Brien was scooping roasted potatoes onto her son's plate with a broad smile. It was Sunday, the day the two of them always had dinner together, and she made it obvious that it was her favorite day of the week. The love and pride she felt for her only son was insurmountable.

"So, how are things with the girls, Jimmy?"

He groaned internally at the question, but he didn't let on that he didn't care to discuss it. Every time he was with his mother, she managed to worm in some kind of question about his love life, and he simply toughed it out. This time was no different.

"No girls, Mom," he replied. "I don't have time, and besides, like I always say, my job is way too dangerous to think about it right now. What would happen if I was hurt or killed on the job? I leave a grieving wife, that's what."

Luciana growled a bit under her breath. "Jimmy, life is too short. A grown woman will know what she is getting herself into, and if she loves you, it won't matter." She put a thick slab of meatloaf on his plate.

He cut a large bite but paused to answer her before

eating it. "I told you before, once I get a promotion and get off the beat, I will start thinking about marriage. Until then…"

"I'm not saying anything about marriage!" She placed a large, cold glass of milk before him and took her own seat. "Just go on a few dates. What could that hurt?" Luciana knew he was lonely. She could feel his loneliness as if it were her own. "If you met the right girl, would you at least go on a date with her?"

Jimmy shrugged as he chewed his meatloaf. "Yeah, I suppose," he said. "I just don't want to rush anything. I'm up for the detective's position that is coming open in six months when Jack Rogers retires. I suppose dating isn't out of the question."

Luciana smiled at him and dropped the subject. Instead, she brought up the church. Jimmy had not attended with her in a while, but she never nagged at him to do so. She simply filled him in on the sermons he missed and who she saw and talked to. The sermon that day had been about letting God change you as you walked with Him instead of trying to change yourself. Her eyes lit up when she talked, so he always gave her his rapt attention, even though it wasn't his favorite topic.

"Oh," she suddenly said in an excited voice. "I saw a couple of people today I haven't seen in years! Years, Jimmy! First I saw Kathy Watkins; remember her? She used to work at the dime store on Felix?"

He thought for a moment. "Large woman? Dark hair? Always wore a dress no matter what? Whatever happened to her anyway?"

"She moved to Washington State to help her daughter with her grandchildren after her daughter got sick with cancer," she replied. "Well, her daughter is cancer free, and after being gone nearly five years, Kathy has come back, but it's only to visit. She will be selling her small house and moving back there permanently."

Jimmy swallowed and washed his food down with milk. "Well, I'm glad to hear her daughter survived cancer."

Luciana nodded. "Oh, yes, I almost forgot," she continued. "I also saw…"

Just then the doorbell rang. Jimmy looked at his mother and noticed her eyes were wide, and he didn't understand the look. "Were you expecting someone, Mom?"

Luciana just shrugged and started to eat her food furiously. Jimmy was now really confused; it seemed she was dodging him somehow. The doorbell rang again, twice this time, and he tossed his napkin on the table and pushed his chair back.

"I guess I'll get that then," he said.

His mother nodded without looking at him. "Yes, dear, go ahead."

Jimmy gave her a confused look before finally heading for the door. Something was off; it seemed his mother was a little too chipper, and that wasn't normal for her. Not unless Matias Garcia was around; then she was beside herself. But Jimmy recognized, without a doubt, that this wasn't the same thing.

He reached the door and opened it to see a very, very pretty blonde woman standing in front of him. She was obviously nervous, hopping slightly from foot to foot. She smiled broadly, revealing straight, pearly white teeth. Her hair was long, with large waves and curls in it, and her eyes were a stunning shade of blue. Jimmy froze immediately.

It was Melody Chapman.

"Hi, Jimmy. How are you?" she began timidly. "Your mother invited me for supper tonight. I know I'm a bit late, and I apologize."

His mouth hung open, and his heart skipped a beat. When he realized that he was standing there looking stupid, he jerked his mind to the here and now. "I'm sorry," he said. "Melody! Wow! She hadn't told me, but it's awesome to see you!"

He held his arms out wide, inviting her to embrace him, and she jumped at the chance. They hugged for a moment, then Jimmy stood back, his hands on her shoulders, and just looked at her, taking her in. He was surprised speechless.

"You... you look amazing!" he said.

Melody blushed, and her eyelids fluttered with embarrassment. "You do too, Jim. Your mother told me you are doing very well. I'm so glad."

He stood there staring for a moment longer before he finally took her by the arm. "Mom is in the kitchen. She invited you, huh? Wow, she hadn't said anything."

"I think she must have wanted it to be a surprise,"

Melody replied.

Jimmy nodded. "Well, she certainly managed that, didn't she! Mom, your dinner guest is here!"

When they walked into the kitchen, Luciana was up and was nearly finished making a plate for the woman. She turned, beaming, and set it down at the empty chair next to Jimmy's. Next, she came around and embraced the girl before saying, "Thank you so much for coming. I have been so excited for you and Jimmy to catch up on old times you know."

Jimmy pulled out the chair for Melody and soon they were all seated. Now he found he was too nervous to eat, and it was all he could do to sit still and keep his demeanor. He didn't know what to say or how to say it.

Finally, he turned to Luciana. "Mom, you should have told me Melody was coming for dinner." He had a smile plastered to his face, but he was giving his mother a look that only she would be able to read.

She smiled at him sweetly and said, "That was what I was saying just as she rang. I ran into Melody at church today!" Luciana reached across the table and gave the girl's arm a firm squeeze. "She just moved back from Los Angeles, Jimmy. I thought it would be wonderful to welcome her home properly!"

Jimmy had finally gotten himself together enough to pick up his fork and put some food on it. "Well! I'm glad to hear that," he replied. "You didn't like L.A.?"

Melody was nervously pushing her meatloaf around on her plate. She gave half a smile and muttered, "Um, it wasn't that. I, uh, just went through a divorce and coming home felt like the right thing to do."

His face went serious instantly. "Oh… I'm sorry. I'm at a loss for words."

Her smile grew, and she shook her head vigorously. "No! Don't be sorry. It was bound to happen. Both of us knew it wasn't right from the start. It's a relief that it's over, really."

He returned her grin. "Kids?"

"No," she answered. "That's the best aspect. No children got hurt."

The three of them began eating, and silence took over for a short while. Of course, Melody had gotten a late start, so once Jimmy was done, he stood and began rinsing his dishes and making small talk with his mother. It didn't take the women long to finish their meals, and Jimmy began to run dishwater and start the clean-up process.

"Jimmy," his mother said as he filled the sink. "We have dessert. I'll take care of that. You sit down while I get the cheesecake."

Within twenty-minutes time, the dessert plates were clear, and the three of them sat chatting with steaming cups of coffee. They reminisced, laughed and joked, and got to know each other all over again, especially Jimmy and Melody. His mother knew her from high school and prom and had always liked the girl, but she didn't know her like Jimmy did. He was pleased to discover that, aside from maturing, she hadn't changed much as a person.

Around 8:30, Luciana stood from the table with her

empty coffee cup in hand. "Well," she began. "I am certainly tired tonight! It has been a long day." She rinsed her cup out and set it next to the neatly stacked dishes beside the sink. "I'll take care of these tomorrow, kids, so don't you worry about them."

With that, she kissed her son, hugged their guest, and announced that she was going to bed. Soon she was gone, and Jimmy sat nervously, as did his old high school girlfriend.

After a full two minutes of silence, he turned to her. "So, do you want to help me do my mother's dirty dishes?" He was smiling playfully, just trying to break the silence.

Melody laughed with relief. "I would love to."

For the rest of the night, they cleaned, joked, and talked about their lives. After his mother went to bed, it didn't take Jimmy long to become completely at ease with the beautiful young woman he was visiting with, and as far as he could tell, she had relaxed just as much. It was the best night he had in a long time.

When he discovered she had walked to dinner, he was more than eager to walk her home. It was just like back in high school: a full moon, a warm evening, and beautiful stars in the sky. When they reached her parents' house, they stopped, and she turned to him to thank him.

"I was scared to see you tonight, Jimmy," she said. "We have gotten older, and life has happened, you know? But I am really glad that I came."

"Me too."

She shrugged and smiled. "Maybe we could get together again? I'll be living here for the next couple of months, at least."

He nodded and looked into her blue eyes. "I'd really like that. Should I call?"

"Yes, please do."

With that, she went inside, and she was gone. Jimmy stood on the porch for a moment or two to clear his head and digest the last few hours. The reality was that he was ecstatic and excited. Melody Chapman! It was perfect.

He went back to his mother's and fetched his car so he could drive himself home. He thought about Melody for the rest of the night, and it made it hard to sleep. When he finally did, he dreamed of her as well.

It was one of the best night's sleep of his life.

∞

Jimmy and Melody sat on the front porch swing at Jimmy's house. It was dusk, and there was a nice warm breeze blowing through her hair. Jimmy gazed at her lovingly, unbeknownst to her, and he knew that he couldn't imagine life without her.

They had been dating now for just over five months. Jimmy had already caught himself, on numerous occasions, daydreaming of asking her to be his wife. He would envision their wedding taking place on a bright, sunny day, with all of their close friends and loved ones in attendance. He would move her into his home, carrying her over the threshold on their first night together, then they would leave the very next day for the tropics to celebrate their nuptials. Yes, Henry James O'Brien was deeply smitten, for the second time in his life, with Melody Chapman.

Melody was staring at the sky with a peaceful look on her face. He thought she must be the most beautiful woman in the world, and he couldn't dream of ever being with another. As he watched her though, her brow knit, and a concerned look came over her face.

"Jimmy…" she began.

At the sound of her voice, he reached up and began to gently stroke her hair. "Yes?"

Without looking at him, she continued. "I have been thinking a lot lately. What is it we are doing? I mean, really. What is this to you?"

The stroking stopped, and he straightened his posture. "Well, I love you, Melody. I've told you that. You know that."

She nodded and sat back. "Well, I can't believe I'm saying this, but I have been thinking about taking this to the next level."

Jimmy was silent for only a moment; that was all it took for him to let her words sink in. "Mel, you know I am not comfortable making such an important commitment while I am still on the beat."

She nodded and finally turned to him. "Yes, you have talked with me about that before, and early on it made sense. But the fact of the matter is, no matter what your position on the force, it will always be dangerous. It sounds like a mere excuse at this point to me, Jim."

He turned her words over briefly in his mind. "Well, maybe it is, but I don't mean for it to be. I think about marrying you all the time."

"Then when?" she asked. "I want a family and a home, and I want those things with you."

Jimmy began to stroke her golden locks once again. "I want the same. That is all I want, too."

"Then when Jim."

He took a deep breath. "You know the detective position is coming open in less than four weeks, and I am the first up. When it comes through, we will begin to make plans."

Her eyes searched his face as she looked for even the slightest trace of either apprehension or dishonesty; she found none. "So, I can expect to be getting a proposal from you soon?" She was smiling, and it made his heart skip a beat.

"You can count on it," he replied. "I just want to be sure I am not marrying you just to leave you or be a burden because I become disabled."

"Jimmy, marrying you would be my decision. Do you think I am not aware of the risk?" she asked. "That is what being married is all about: for better or worse."

He nodded. "I know, Mel. Just let me get the promotion and that better salary. It will be for the best, not only for us, but for any little Jimmies or Mellies that come along, okay?"

Satisfied, Melody took his arm and draped it over her own shoulders, then snuggled against him. Jimmy kissed her on the head, and the two of them sat that way, silent and satisfied, for the next hour. It was the most content and happy he had ever been, and even though he was apprehensive and concerned, he found himself eager for his promotion to come through. Whether he had stress over it or not, Jimmy O'Brien was ready to get on with the next phase of his life.

He was ready to really live.

R.W.K. Clark

CHAPTER 12

Jimmy drove to the station, enjoying the bright sun as it beat down on his face. It was a warm morning, but not too hot, and he had the windows down so he could feel the air on his skin. Today he would be meeting with Matias to discuss his promotion. The detective who was leaving, Kurt McIntyre, would be retiring in one week. Matias had called Jimmy in for a meeting, and he could only presume it was in regards to the pending transition.

He parked his car in the designated lot and got out, locking it up securely out of sheer habit. He hummed to himself as he made his way into the station. It had been a great year so far, and things were about to get better very, very soon. It was all he could do to not sing out loud.

Inside, he checked his mailbox, then made sure there were no telephone messages for him. Once he was all clear on both, he made his way to Chief Garcia's office. The door was closed, and Jimmy could hear him talking on the other side of the door, so he plopped down in one of the three chairs lined up just outside the office door.

After about ten minutes, he heard the chief hang up

his telephone, so Jimmy stood and rapped lightly on the door.

"Yes?" the chief hollered.

Jimmy turned the knob and opened it, poking his head through. "It's just me, Mat."

"Jimmy! Come in, come in," he replied. "I all but completely forgot you were on your way. How's the little lady?"

Jimmy stepped in, closed the door, and sat in the chair across from Matias. "She's good," he said. "With the promotion coming, we are actually tossing around the idea of taking things to the next level, believe it or not."

"Ah, it's good to hear that. Just give me a second, here," Mat continued. "I want to let Janice know to hold my calls and stop interruptions for a bit." He picked up his phone and punched in a few numbers to reach his secretary.

Jimmy noticed that the chief's eyes were terribly bloodshot. He looked more tired than usual, and his handsome face appeared very old and worn out. He had been drinking more and more in the last year, Jimmy knew. The job was getting to him, and he had tried to talk to his mother about it, knowing how close she and Matias had become. Unfortunately, Luciana had been unwilling to discuss it. She was one of the most loyal human beings he knew, and if she cared for someone, she would not speak ill behind his back. He dropped it, but today he was wondering if he shouldn't bring it up again, this time with Matias himself present.

The chief spoke to his secretary briefly, then hung up and focused his full attention on Jimmy, offering him a weak smile. "So, glad you came in on your day off, Jim. You know I appreciate the way you always go the extra mile. You're looking forward to your promotion, are you?"

Jimmy laughed heartily. "Of course! It means I can begin to expand on my personal life a bit, finally." He shifted in his chair a bit. "A few weeks ago, Mel brought it up herself. I mean, I'm nervous, and I've had my reasons for dodging the issue, I guess, but if I want to keep her, I'm going to have to do the right thing. This promotion couldn't be coming at a more perfect time."

Matias nodded and stood from his desk. He paced a bit with his hands clasped behind his back, stopping only to gaze out the window every now and then. Jimmy could tell that the man had some things on his mind, and he knew he was getting ready to find out just what they were.

"I know that you are aware of the fact that my drinking has gotten somewhat... out of control," Matias began. He turned to Jimmy. "Am I correct?"

Jimmy shrugged, unsure of how he should answer. He finally decided that honesty, coupled with tact, was the best policy with this man whom he loved and knew so well. He weighed his words carefully.

"Um, yes, I suppose so."

The chief started to pace again, obviously being careful with his own words. "Well, your mother is very concerned, as I'm sure you are, and to be honest, I'm a bit worried myself. You do know that I love Luciana very much, don't you Jim?"

Jimmy knew that they were close, but he had never considered that they may have a deep affection for each other of that sort. He thought about it and decided that he should not be surprised. They had both been single for many years, they both loved him, and they were already best friends. It was perfect, actually.

"I guess I did," he finally replied.

"Well, like you and Melody, I wanted to talk to your mom about marriage," Matias continued. "I mean, it is the logical next step, at least it is to me, anyway."

The man began to shake his head as he paced. "When I brought it up last Friday, she brought up the drinking. She is worried, both for me and for what it would do to our relationship if we wed. Luciana knows that my job is basically killing me. What, with having just arrested three dirty officers in the last two months, and with the crime rate skyrocketing like it has. Not to mention all the coke that is in Bernalillo now. Well, to make a long story short, your mother won't marry me unless I retire and get the booze under control."

"Um, I don't know what you want me to say, Mat," Jimmy said. He began to fidget nervously now. "I love my mother, and I want what's best for her. If she is concerned though, I have to consider that. I mean, she is the most level-headed person in the world. She wouldn't say it if it weren't true."

Matias nodded and sat back down in his chair. "I know that, Jimmy. I know. Luciana is the only light in my dark life, and I am not willing to give that up; not now, not ever."

Jimmy remained silent and watched the chief carefully. After a moment, the man took a deep, ragged breath and continued. "That's why I am going to pull retirement."

An alarmed look came over Jimmy's face, and his stomach trembled inside. "Retirement? You wouldn't even retire when it was time, Mat." He thought for a moment longer. He wasn't questioning that retirement was best, both for Mat and his mother. He was wondering how it would affect him, and that was selfish. "It's for the best, I'm sure. So, when will this happen?"

Mat cleared his throat and looked Jimmy in the eyes, his own bloodshot ones glowing. "Next week, Jim."

His mind could not wrap around what he was hearing. So soon? "Who will be stepping up?"

"You will."

"Me?" It was Jimmy's turn to stand and pace. "But I haven't even made detective! There are far more qualified men who are likely waiting on that. Shouldn't they be up? This is going to piss off a lot of people!"

Mat shook his head. "No. No, it isn't. No one is more qualified or more trustworthy. Those three cops we busted? Two of them would have been next in line. They extorted and stole. They couldn't be trusted. Who's next? The only one I am sure isn't next... well, that's you."

"But... but..."

"Jim, I met with most of the men today, and all of them feel you are the right man for the job," Mat said quietly. "All of them."

Jimmy stopped pacing for a moment and looked up at the chief. "So, I am going to begin filling your shoes next week. No detective position at all. What about training?"

"You'll attend some evening classes for one week every month in Albuquerque as your ongoing education," Mat replied. "Expenses paid of course. They will also cover in-depth investigation, et cetera."

Jimmy felt as though the wind had been knocked out of him. He didn't know why he felt so unsure, so frightened. This was exactly what he had worked for his entire life, and it just fell into his lap directly from the sky. So why did he suddenly want to run from it?

He wasn't ready, that was the reason, and he knew it. He planned to work his way up, slowly get promoted, and learn everything he could to be a great Chief. What if he couldn't do it?

"You can do this, Jim," Mat said as though he were reading his mind. "I talked to your mother about it, and even she knows you are ready. I can see by your face that you don't think you are, but I assure you, you are the only one who thinks that. Everything I do, you are more than capable of doing, and you will excel at it. Jimmy, I've known this since you were a boy."

A misty look came into Mat's bloodshot eyes, and he smiled slightly, as though reminiscing. "You were born to do this. It is your destiny."

Jimmy plopped back down into the chair he had been sitting in. His hands were trembling, and he was finding it difficult to breathe. Mat said nothing, only watched Jimmy closely and gave him the time he needed. After five minutes, Jimmy finally spoke.

"What if I refuse?"

Now it was Mat's turn to give a hearty laugh. "Why would you do that? It's been your vision your entire life, now here it is. So, it's a bit premature, but only in your mind. So what? Refusing is the craziest thing I've ever heard come out of your mouth, and you are not a crazy man."

Jimmy put his head in his hands and stared at the floor. Maybe Mat was right. Maybe he was unsure only because it wasn't what he expected, what he had planned. Perhaps he was more ready for this than he thought, but he certainly wasn't positive that was all the way true.

"Well, then," Mat continued, standing from his chair once again. "You will be sworn in for the position at a ceremony being held at three in the afternoon next Thursday. There will, of course, be a small celebration afterward. I'll be there, as will your mother, Melody, and most everyone else on the force who is not on duty. You will begin actually working the following Monday."

He patted his growing stomach and groaned. "I'll be having a retirement party on Friday, the next day. Your mother is throwing it, and it will be at La Quinta Mexican Restaurant. I assume you and Melody will be there?"

"Yeah, Mat. Sure thing," Jimmy replied absently.

The chief walked around the desk and put his hands on the shoulders of a dazed Jimmy. As he stood behind him, he said, "I'm proud of you, kid, and I have the utmost faith in you. You are my son, as far as I am concerned, and I love ya, Jimmy."

Suddenly, Jimmy felt like he was suffocating. The room was spinning, and all he could think about was getting outside and getting some fresh air. He reached up and gave one of Mat's hands a pat.

"Well, I think I'm gonna head home and process all of this." He stood up and turned to his friend and mentor. "I love you too, Mat. I hope you are making the right decision."

The man gave another laugh, his eyes lit with amusement. "Jimmy, if you have ever trusted me in your life, trust me on this."

He left the Chief's Office, realizing clearly that it would soon be his own. It felt like all eyes in the place were on him, and a quick look around confirmed it. Most were even smiling, but he only nodded at each of them in return. He didn't want to talk about the subject with anyone yet because he just wasn't ready. Obviously, he had been the last to find out, and he needed to digest what he had just learned.

He stepped outside into the sunlight and immediately squinted against its bright glare. The heat struck him too, and he began to walk briskly toward his car, fingering through his keys in search of the right one as he walked. Soon he was steering in the direction of his house, his mind going a million miles an hour. He had planned to mow the yard, but now he knew he would need a couple of hours of peace before he tackled that job.

At home, in the air-conditioned comfort, he lay on the sofa and allowed his mind to think about his upcoming promotion as much as it desired. Now was the time to adjust, and now was the time to accept the massive change. His life was getting ready to change more than he could comprehend.

Maybe, now was also the time to get a ring and propose to Mel; it would certainly knock her off her feet.

∞

Two hundred ninety miles away Kevin Marshall sat in the sweltering heat of a broken down warehouse located in Juarez, Mexico at the exact moment Jimmy O'Brien was being told he would soon be chief. Kevin sat at his typical spot at a long folding table which was always used for meetings like this one, meetings held to update the employees of Pedro Rodriguez.

Pedro Rodriguez was one of the most powerful cartel bosses in Mexico, and being consistent with updates was a vital part of the business for him. Not only did he want to know exactly what was going on with his business at all times, but he also wanted his employees to know what they needed to know as well. This meeting was no different than any of the others. All of the updating and filling in was complete. Now, in the front of the room, a cartel worker by the name of

Raul Martinez was in a folding chair with two of Rodriguez's heavy men on either side of him. Rodriguez himself sat in a comfortable desk chair, his arms resting on the leather covered chair arms provided.

He was a fat man with his long hair slicked back and wore a black button-down shirt that was sweatstained. He smiled an evil smile as he questioned Martinez, and he waited with the patience of a lion about ready to dine for the answers the man was giving.

"You know, Raul, how much I appreciate the work you have managed to do in Bernalillo?" The boss began to play with a black ink pen, looking at it and smiling as he did so.

Beads of sweat were on the man's face, and his eyes were wide with both fear and uncertainty. "Yuh-yes, Mr. Rodriguez, sir."

Pedro Rodriguez continued to smile and began spinning around in his chair as he spoke. "Ah, yes. It was important to become established there. I trusted you to get things going and growing, and you did."

Martinez nodded vigorously, sweat flying from his face.

"Now I hear rumors, you see," Rodriguez continued. "Rumors that you are taking what is mine from behind my back. I ask you if this is true, and you deny it. Is this all correct, Raul Martinez?"

The nodding continued.

"Answer me!" Pedro screamed, his eyes on fire.

Now Raul's entire body began to shake violently, his flesh trembling on his heavy frame. "Yes, yes, it is correct, sir."

"What if I tell you that I have proof, Martinez. What if I tell you I have a witness to your stealing, and that witness is in this very place right now?"

Raul Martinez began to cry immediately, blubbering like a small boy who had just received the spanking of his life.

Pedro Rodriguez stood from his chair and tossed his pen on the folding table. The sick smile was still plastered to his face as he approached Raul and the two heavies standing by him. He began to speak to the petrified man in a soft, soothing voice.

"Oh, Raul. Raul, Raul, Raul," he said as he walked around behind the man. He put his hands on the man's shoulders and began to massage them gently. "Stop your blubbering. You do all this to yourself."

Raul continued sobbing, but he nodded in response.

"Let me see... how much did you take? No! Don't answer that, Martinez. I never ask a question I do not already know the answer to," Pedro said. "So far you steal four million American dollars from my operation. MY OPERATION!"

With that, he curled his fist and punched the man at the base of his neck with all his might. The blow immediately knocked the wind out of him, and his crying and wailing stopped as he gasped for air. Pedro ignored his struggle and walked around until he was facing him. He knelt down and watched as the man tried to breathe, and he began to laugh uncontrollably at the sight.

When Raul Martinez finally was able to take in a breath of air, Pedro Rodriguez did not hesitate. "I will tell your wife and boys that you love them, you no good piece of shit." He took the gun from the man on his right and blew Raul Martinez's head off without so much as a flinch. Then, he handed the gun back to the man and said, "You two clean this pile of crap up. It is beginning to stink."

Kevin Marshall, along with the other four men at the table, began to wipe sweat from their foreheads and struggled to keep their food down. Rodriguez paid them no mind, though. Instead, he walked calmly back to the table, picked up his ink pen, and sat back down in his leather chair. He then resumed spinning around as he began to speak.

"Once those two have him out of here, you all may go," he said in a deadly quiet voice. "Let this be yet another lesson to you: I will not be taken for a fool, ever!"

In less than five minutes, the dead man who had been working Bernalillo, New Mexico was gone, and only blood and tissue dripping down a far wall remained. All of the men stood to leave, except for Pedro Rodriguez, of course. He was still playing with his pen and spinning around in his chair.

Without looking up, he suddenly said, "Kevin Marshall, you stay!"

Kevin stopped suddenly and jerked around, a confused and frightened look on his face. "Sir?"

He slowly made his way back to his place at the

folding table, thoughts of bullets and brains dancing morbidly in his head. He frantically reviewed all of his behavior to see if he had done anything worth assassination, and the only thing he could think of was coming up with the idea to take the business to Bernalillo nearly fifteen years ago when he was just a pup at eighteen. With the events of the day regarding Raul Martinez and the stealing, he was sure he would be eating a bullet in the next few minutes or so, and his blood was running cold.

"Sit, sit, Marshall," Pedro Rodriguez said with a wave of his hand. At the order, Kevin dropped into the cold folding chair that, moments before had been warm.

Pedro spun in his chair one final time before throwing his pen across the room and looking Kevin in the eye. "How long have I known you, Kevin?"

With trembling hands and heart, Kevin replied, "Nearly fifteen years, sir. Since I was eighteen. At least, that's when I met you face to face."

The boss began to rub his chin. "You used to sell for me on a second-hand basis, yes? You used to get the stuff from Pablo Castillo in south Albuquerque, yes?"

"Yes, sir."

"I remember now," the man continued with a smile on his face. "You were arrested for selling out of your school. Did you know, some of the men I had on the inside at the time kept their eyes on you, and they gave me full reports? Never once did you bring up Pablo's name to the pigs. Never once."

"No, sir."

Rodriguez stood and walked over to pick up his pen. The man always played with a pen, sometimes even chewing on it. One of the other men had told Kevin years ago that having a pen helped Rodriguez to think. He was not surprised when the boss went to retrieve the one that he had thrown.

"I kept tabs on you the whole time they kept you locked up, and I knew when they let you out," he continued. "And then, I sent Marcus Dawson from Santa Fe down to recruit you. The kind of loyalty you possess that is the kind of loyalty I want and need, Kevin Marshall."

Kevin remained quiet, waiting for his boss to continue.

"Now we have Raul, who is no more than a bloody meat sack," he said. "He stole, and he wouldn't know what loyalty meant if it ran through his heart like a knife. Would he, now?"

"No, sir."

Pedro shook his head. "No, sir, indeed. But that is neither here nor there, Kevin Marshall. I have a much more pressing issue at hand at the current time, and that is why I ask you to stay."

Kevin kept his eyes on the man as he went quiet and began spinning around rapidly in his chair once again. He was gnawing on the cap of his pen now, and Kevin could see clearly that he was deep in thought. He nearly jumped out of his skin when the chair abruptly stopped, and Rodriguez leaned forward toward him.

"This issue is that I have no one running things in

Bernalillo any longer."

He let that sink into Kevin's brain. It didn't need to; Kevin knew exactly why he made him stay as soon as the words were out of his mouth. He wanted him to take over operations in Bernalillo, New Mexico, and the surrounding area.

"I'm listening, sir."

Once again the man stood, only this time he walked until he was directly across the table from the man, then he sat down in one of the cold metal chairs. He wove his pen back and forth between his fingers but kept his eyes closely on Kevin.

"You are from there," he said. "You know the town, and all around it, very well, yes?"

Kevin nodded. "Of course."

"You know people, lots of people?"

"You know that I do, sir," he replied. "But for the last fifteen or so years, I have lived here, working for you."

Rodriguez waved off his words. "This I know, but I need someone there right now. Someone I can depend on to make good numbers. Someone who knows how business is done and recognizes a good sales target when he sees it," he said. "Someone who is LOYAL."

Kevin drew a deep breath. "Well, I guess that would be me, sir."

The man smiled and sat back. "Yes, I guess that would be you."

He nodded solemnly at his boss. There was no need to think or even try to argue. No, he had come too far with the organization to let fear or nervousness take over.

CHAPTER 13

Jimmy looked out over the seemingly endless dunes of pure white sand, and he reveled in the most powerful feelings of serenity and smallness that he had ever known or dreamed to exist. He had always wanted to visit the White Sands National Monument, but his mother worked so much and had so little money, that it hadn't been possible. Even as a young man, he had been so focused on his future career, and then his career itself, that his intent to visit somehow slipped both his mind and his grasp.

It was Sunday now. They would leave on Monday morning, after being there since Saturday afternoon. It had been a spur of the moment thing; Melody had remembered him talking about visiting White Sands way back in high school. When she asked him about it on Friday afternoon, right after she accepted his proposal to marry him, he told her he never had made it there, no matter how badly he had wanted to. Other things had simply… gotten in the way.

Now here they stood, both of them breathless and speechless from the sight before them. It was almost as beautiful as Mel's face when she said 'Yes!' Even she was purer in his eyes, and being there right then with her made it all the more worthwhile.

Inevitably, he smiled to himself and thought back to Friday. He had left Garcia's office and sat in the silence of his vehicle for over ninety minutes. Sometimes he had run the air conditioner to keep cool, others he simply turned it off and rolled down the window, but he sat there. He made himself look at all the benefits of being chief for so long that soon it was all he could see, so he finally started his car, turned the radio on, and drove to Mangold's Jewelers, right there in Bernalillo.

Jimmy had plenty of money; for so long had he been alone that all he did was put it in the bank, pay his meager bills, and work. When he walked through the door of that shop, he was fresh meat for the salespersons, and he knew it. He didn't care what he spent, because he was going to pay cash that day, and he was going to make some employee's month.

He chose a dainty platinum wedding set. The engagement band had a matte surface, and it appeared to be wrapped with diamonds, placed in a thin spiral around the tiny band. It was set off with a center diamond that was two carats, and it had 'petals' of tiny diamonds around it.

The wedding band itself had nothing but the spiral of diamonds around it, and they were staggered from the diamonds on the engagement band; that way they complemented each other, seemingly hugging, becoming one ring.

She was due to come over that night to watch the

news, have dinner, and spend the rest of the evening watching reruns. It was then that he intended to tell her about his promotion… and ask for her hand in marriage. He left the jewelry store literally whistling.

For their supper, he prepared something he knew she would love far more than seafood or steak; he made hamburgers and French fries done in the deep fryer. She loved wine, so he bought her a cheap bottle of Merlot, and he lit a candle on the coffee table so they could watch TV while they ate.

She was like no one else. Jimmy could completely be himself around her, and now that he was getting that promotion, he knew he could safely (knock on wood) make her his wife. He wasn't going to make excuses and let anyone steal her away because he had been too slow on the draw.

She had shown up two minutes early, at 5:58. They watched the news, and the food kept warm for thirty minutes in the oven. Afterward, they ate, and finally, after the second episode, Jimmy turned the sound on the television down and turned to Melody.

"So, how was your day?" he had asked.

She had smiled up at him, her eyes misty with affection. "It was long," she replied.

"That rough, huh?"

"Only until I got here and saw you…"

They had kissed, and he proceeded to tell her about the news he had received from Chief Garcia, the news that he would be chief in a week. Melody had come unglued with joy, and it had taken him twenty minutes to calm her down enough for him to pop the question.

No matter how hard he tried, it wasn't going to work that way. He no more reached into his pocket for the white velvet box then she had him figured out. Once again, she lost all emotional control, and he wouldn't even let her see the ring until she reined herself in.

Finally, he was able to ask and offer her the ring, and she accepted in a giddy state of tears.

Now it was Sunday, and they were on a spontaneous trip to White Sands. They intended to marry on Friday since he would be sworn in on Thursday and put off their honeymoon for a while in favor of a short weekend together initially. He would start as chief, and they would jump into the flow of their lives right away. When they got home, they would call the few family and friends they wanted to invite, take care of the marriage license and any other requirements, and they would be married by Judge Haskins at the courthouse.

He was fully happy. He was at White Sands. In only days he would marry his dream girl, Melody, and by the beginning of next week, he would start as Chief Henry James O'Brien of the Bernalillo Police Department.

He couldn't imagine that life could ever get better than this.

∞

Kevin Marshall steered the brand new SUV smoothly along Interstate 25. He had just crossed the border minutes before, and now it would be smooth sailing all the way home, to Bernalillo. He smiled to himself; it certainly helped that he was completely comfortable. He had a new SUV, new clothes, a place waiting for him in Bernalillo, and plenty of cash to live on. What more could a man ask for? Nothing, except for maybe good pussy.

Soon he would be back in the old hometown, back in the old 'homestead,' as it was called when he was a kid. He knew most wouldn't remember him right off, and he knew it. He was okay with that; the longer it took, the better. The one thing that made him understand that coming back was the right decision, not just for him, but for Pedro Rodriguez, was the fact that most of the locals had put him completely out of their minds.

His parents had moved to Florida right after he got out of the 'juvie joint.' They gave him five grand and told him to make his own way; then they promptly kicked him to the curb. Kevin hadn't spoken to them or hardly thought about them, ever since. He had made his own way, and they had nothing to do with it. He was his own man, no matter how his road went or how it ended.

He continued to drive, completely relaxed and confident. The radio blared heavy metal music, and he bobbed his head up and down to the beat. The drive went smoothly and without incident. It sure did help to have a nice, new vehicle with legitimate plates. Rodriguez had always managed to take really good care of him, especially when he went above and beyond with his work.

He never had been strung out on coke. Now, that wasn't to say he had never used it. He just did it so occasionally that it hardly really counted as real 'use.' Maybe twice a year he would indulge, and if he had to work, he would never even think about it. He knew that Rodriguez was aware of this. More than one of his colleagues had mentioned that the boss had asked them why they couldn't control themselves, the way Marshall does. He wore that proudly, like a badge, but in humble silence.

Soon Kevin saw the sign: Bernalillo: 7 miles.

It was enough to make him sit up straight in his seat and turn the radio off so he could concentrate. It almost made him feel like he had done something wrong, and that was a very uncomfortable feeling. He quickly pulled himself together and set his focus; he would be there soon, for it was but a stone's throw away.

Kevin grabbed a single sheet of lined paper off the passenger seat; on it was the address of his new apartment. 5336 Pueblo Place. The last he had known Pueblo Place had gone up only to the thirty-five-hundred block; after that, it was nothing but outskirts and desert. The town must have grown more than he could've imagined.

Despite his concerns, he arrived in Bernalillo as if on a cloud. He drove through the town wondering at the changes, but he took close notice of all that had virtually remained unchanged as well. It didn't take him but mere minutes to locate Pueblo Place, and soon after that, he found himself approaching a new development on the outer edges of the town he had once called home. A fast food restaurant had been built catty-corner from the Pueblo La Casa Apartments, and a brand new Quickmart gas station was all lit up just across the street. He could hardly breathe; it was much like waking up and finding yourself in the Twilight Zone. He could hardly wait to see Bernalillo in the daytime.

There was a main driveway into the Pueblo La Casa Apartments, a split drive consisting of both an entrance and an exit. The landscaping was immaculate, and only the most recent models of cars were parked in the perfectly marked spaces. Garages were lined up behind some of the buildings, but others offered only spaces.

He easily found building '5336'. He was not surprised to find that his building had a garage; that explained the extra key on his chain. Rodriguez was a firm believer that the way his employees lived was a direct reflection on him, so only the best was to be expected. His apartment was 'A,' and as soon as he found the garage unit with an 'A' above it, he parked his car safely inside.

Next, he made his way to the building. His unit was on the ground floor, much to his delight. He had always hated being a pest to those around him, as far as his personal life went. This would ensure he could live quietly and draw minimal attention to his own existence. So far, Kevin Marshall could not have been happier.

He unlocked the heavy oak door and swung it open. The light switch was directly to the left, and he found it quickly and easily. With nothing more than a flip,

Kevin's breath was stolen from him.

The apartment was fully furnished with lots of black, glass, and brass. A massive big-screen television was the focal point of the room, and Kevin noticed the tell-tale sign of Surround Sound by the speakers hanging in various spots, high on the walls.

All of the décor complimented the furnishings beautifully. Modern pieces that Kevin was sure were prints, yet he knew that Rodriguez had spent an abundant amount of money on them. He simply stood in the doorway shaking his head in disbelief.

After taking in the rest of the place, the massive bedroom with its king-sized bed, the bathroom with its sunken bath and hot tub, and all of the incredible closet space, Kevin decided it was time to get his things inside and make it official. He didn't have much; just an oversized duffle bag stuffed full of clothing and a smaller one with his personal hygiene items. He had also brought some of his favorite music; Rodriguez and most of the other boys had tastes that leaned toward more Latin sounds, but Kevin loved to head-bang.

He went back out to the garage, appreciating the good night-time lighting of his new residence, and grabbed his things. Back inside it took him all of twenty minutes to unpack and put things neatly away, just the way he liked them. He had two handguns, both of which he wasn't sure where to store. As he searched each and every closet and cubby in the house, he was pleased to discover a washer and dryer behind one set of doors, and he made a mental note to buy laundry soap.

Finally, he decided to keep the guns in the drawer of the nightstand furthest from the bedroom door. Beneath the drawer he discovered a small safe; it was the lockable type, and a small ring with two keys was dangling from the lock itself. He quickly got his trusty shoebox full of cash and put it away. After securing the lock, he put the pair of keys on his keyring and went to have a drink before retiring. He had noticed a small bar in the living area, and if he knew Rodriguez, it would be fully stocked.

He poured himself a double-shot of whiskey, lowered the lights, and sat down to contemplate the following day. It would be a busy one. He needed to touch base with the local troops and find out what page they were all on. They had been made aware that a new boss was being sent, so they were expecting him. The men would have to account to him for all the dope, and they would need to show him numbers that matched. He didn't want to have to bang heads together, but if it was required, well, he did take a certain… pleasure in it.

Once he had the numbers, he would report back to Rodriguez, then he would keep his eyes out for a big yellow TransShip truck. That truck would bring him a large box of cheap stuffed animals, and each of them held a very expensive and addictive secret. He would get all of that in line, and let the games begin.

Yes, tomorrow would be a very busy day indeed.

R.W.K. Clark

CHAPTER 14

Jimmy lay in the darkness in his room listening to the light, steady breathing of the gorgeous woman lying next to him: Mrs. Melody O'Brien. All was very quiet, but for the breathing, except for the occasional groan and fart emitted by Max, the dog at the foot of the bed. He couldn't be in better shape.

The ceremony for his swearing-in was incredible, if not a bit surreal. It went all too quickly. While he was fully aware of the actual process, all he seemed to remember was the multitude of flashbulbs that continued to go off all around him, distracting him and making him flinch. It lasted all of five minutes and was followed by a thundering round of applause offered up by all of his friends and loved ones.

The party afterward was very mild. Only coffee, tea, and pop were served, though later that night, he and all the other officers who were off-duty met at Columbo's Bar and had a few pitchers. No matter how real it all was, he couldn't seem to shake the feeling that he was living in a dream, and he had to fight the urge to pinch himself awake constantly. He had actually gone so far as to attempt a single pinch once, but Melody had caught him. She had gently smacked him and then burst out laughing, knowing what he was doing, and he couldn't help but laugh with her. It was time to accept the situation as being utterly real.

Then, earlier that day, he and Melody had married at the courthouse. In attendance were Melody's parents and younger sister, his mother, Matias Garcia, and the judge. Simple and beautiful, it had been, at least to Jimmy. He knew that Melody was pleased because she glowed like a lightning bug that couldn't shut it off. If either of them had been nervous, no one could tell; it went smoothly and was an event filled with laughter and love.

Afterward, they all went to Garcia's retirement party at La Quinta Mexican Restaurant. It was a time of major celebration, and half the force was in attendance. Fortunately, Luciana had reserved a back room for the party. The group certainly got loud, and they went through an abundance of tequila. Jimmy noticed that Mat had only one margarita; after that, all he could do was stare at Luciana with clouds in his eyes and sip iced tea.

The retirement party also served as a reception for the newlyweds, so it worked out perfectly. Everything seemed absolutely perfect. So perfect, in fact, that Jimmy found himself waiting for the other shoe to drop and ruin everything. But now he was lying in his bed next to his new wife, and all had gone off without a hitch of any kind. It was absolutely wonderful.

He considered their plans for tomorrow. They

would go and pick up the rest of Melody's things from her parents' home, where she had been living. Then they would spend the rest of the evening living like a normal married couple: Jimmy would do yard work while Melody unpacked, settled in, and got the house together. They might do a bit of shopping if she found they lacked anything that would make her move even better. Monday was just around the corner, and there were preparations to be made for that day as well.

Jimmy's eyelids finally began to grow heavy, and the racing thoughts in his mind decided to slow down. He couldn't believe how much his life had changed in the last week, but it had, and now it was time to man up and get into the swing of things. As he dozed off, he felt settled and completely comfortable with his new life.

∞

On Thursday evening Kevin Marshall sat before the big screen television in his living room eating Chinese take-out and drinking a cold beer. He was waiting for the news to come on in ten minutes; it was important to keep up with the local goings on if he was going to run things properly in Bernalillo.

After checking with the troops, he had nothing but good news to report to Rodriguez. For the first time in a long time, the Bernalillo numbers came up on top. Getting rid of Raul Martinez had been very necessary. Kevin wasn't sure how much the man had actually stolen, but it was no wonder to him that Rodriguez had buried a bullet in the man's brain. He had been a dirty liar and thief, and he had been screwing things up but good. Well, Kevin was just the man to make it all right again.

The news began, and an immaculately dressed young woman with red hair, green eyes, and perfect make-up came on the screen. She welcomed the viewers to 'WNMX... New Mexico's Most Reliable News!' Kevin didn't recognize the anchorwoman; he had been gone a long time, and many, many changes had taken place in and around his hometown.

She began by making a few local announcements, and then before cutting to the break, she briefly touched base on the night's top stories. When they returned, they would cover the story of a homeless man who was given a free meal and a job by the owner of a local burger joint after an employee tried to kick him off the property. A junior high teacher has been suspended pending accusations that she has been having sex with a thirteen-year-old student. And a new police chief has had a busy week, being both sworn into his position and married, all within two days.

"All of that and more when we return!" The redhead said, and they cut to commercial.

Kevin stood and took his take-out boxes to the kitchen, along with his empty beer can. He tossed the boxes in the garbage, then smashed the can and threw it away as well before fetching another and returning to the television. The news came back on just as he sat down.

Red-head covered the teacher/molester story first, and it barely held Kevin's attention. He didn't have kids, so what did he care? He only wished he had a female teacher like that in junior high; the only difference was that he would have been the one doing the molesting.

Next, she went over the homeless-man-turned-burger-employee. Kevin waved that away absently and drained half of his beer. They would report anything as long as it took up at least two minutes of their time on the air. He hated watching the news, but it simply had to be done; not doing so could be detrimental to his career and his life.

Next came the story of the new police chief.

At first, Kevin only listened as he thumbed through the TV Guide. The guy not only got sworn in, but he got married, and by golly, he was one busy fellow. They said he was a life-long resident of Bernalillo, and that was enough to make Kevin look up.

He recognized the guy before they even said his name. As a matter of fact, he didn't need them to tell him. It was Jimmy O'Brien, his old elementary school pal. The one who gave him the shove off when he stole money from that whiny girl all those years ago. The one he had picked on throughout junior high and the first years of high school.

The one who had gotten him busted in eleventh grade and made it, so he had to cool his heels in juvie for more than a year and a half.

Kevin could feel his temperature rising, and anger began to boil up from deep down inside of him. He jumped to his feet and walked to the front of the television, and stared up at the large screen, the light flickering on his face. The chief O'Brien. The same guy he had sworn to get, the same guy he had lost sleep over many, many nights in the last fifteen years.

At first, he was beside himself, almost panicking. But it didn't take him long to pull himself together. Rather than be afraid or nervous, he would work this to his advantage. This was the perfect opportunity to take this guy out, once and for all. Jimmy was being handed to him on a silver platter.

He stood up quickly and shook it off. It was time to begin to plan. The good news was, Jimmy O'Brien had a pretty little wife for Kevin to toy with as well. Oh, yes, life was good.

He plopped down on the couch and began letting his wheels freely turn.

CHAPTER 15

"As we all know, our fair little city has been battling the cocaine demon for some years now. An ongoing investigation has given us little to go on, that is, until now." Chief Jimmy O'Brien stood before his men at six-thirty in the morning, briefing them on recent findings and what the focus of both detectives and beat cops would be for the next while.

He had been active as chief for more than two months now, and one of his main focuses was to get the drug trade in Bernalillo under control, hopefully eliminating it if that was at all possible. Since stepping into Matias' shoes, he had begun to really crackdown. Progress had been slow, but two days prior a high school student got caught with three grams of coke, all separately bagged into quarter-grams. This was good news because it meant the kid was dealing, and that meant he had a hookup.

Dane Smith was a local boy whose mother had passed in a car accident when he was six. His father had been raising him, but because he had sought solace in the bottle, he had done a less than desirable job. Now this kid was sixteen years old, and to make a bit of money, he had begun to sling coke at Bernalillo High, and who knew where else.

When he was arrested, it was a fluke; he had been hitting on some girls outside Harver's Grocery, and they had resisted him. He lost control and got handy with one of them, and one of the girls called the police without hesitation. When the cops arrived, he was walking off as if nothing had happened, but the girl already had a large purple bruise on her arm, and she was sobbing uncontrollably.

At the station, he was initially questioned by detectives and one of the arresting officers. They asked him the basic questions: Do you have any more stuff besides this? How long have you been selling? Who is your supplier? The kid answered any questions that incriminated himself; when it came to supplier questions of any kind, he suddenly couldn't hear or seemingly speak English anymore.

Jimmy had observed the entire thing from behind the two-way glass. The more he had watched, the more pissed off he got. Finally, after two hours he knocked on the window, signifying to the other officers to meet him outside the room. He told them he was going to have a shot at the kid and see if he could pry him open. The frustrated detectives let him have a go, of course.

He went into the room with two cans of soda; one for him, and one for the kid. He even broke his own rules and offered him a cigarette, which he had bummed, from one of his officers. The kid took it gratefully and inhaled his first drag as if it contained much-needed life's blood. Jimmy simply watched him and let him relax.

After a few minutes, he finally began. "So, Dane, you know what happens from here, right?"

The kid met his eyes and took another drag. He exhaled, watching the smoke as it drifted toward the ceiling, then looked back at Jimmy. "Yeah, I'm going to juvie. Probably 'til I'm eighteen."

"Well," Jimmy said as he sat forward in his chair. "You're partially right. You'll go to juvie, yes. But because of the recent cocaine rampage, a lot of the laws for juvenile offenders have stiffened recently. They've been going to juvie until eighteen, and then they are transferred to the Penitentiary of New Mexico until they hit the ten-year mark."

The boy's eyes widened, and his hands began to tremble, but he said nothing. Jimmy continued, "You're what, all of sixteen?"

"I'll be seventeen in four months," Dane replied.

"Hmmm. Yep," Jimmy said. "So you'll do right around a year in juvie, then you'll head north and do about nine years. You might get time off if you behave, but you'll still do at least five."

The kid looked like he was going to cry, but he managed to keep the tears from falling. Jimmy felt bad; he was deceiving the kid big time, but he had to do what he had to do. After all, it was a war they were fighting.

"What can I do?" Dane had asked.

Jimmy shrugged. "Not much. I mean, there are some things you can do, but a tough kid like you? Nah,

I bet you're not willing to save your own butt. Funny, because I don't see any of your people down here trying to save it for you."

By the time he was done sweet talking the kid, he had spilled several names of small-time soldiers who were stationed locally. He knew there was one particular guy in charge of the area, but he didn't know his name. He was pretty new, and Dane Smith hadn't met him yet, nor did the other guys mention him by name. All Dane knew was that he was a white guy and he lived in Bernalillo.

Jimmy briefed his boys on all of this. The guy was sneaky, and while he was in charge, he used minions to keep himself under wraps. Jimmy made them aware that this new local boss was in no way the kingpin. No, he was but a minion himself. The goal was to get to the main man, but in the meantime, they were going to focus on tracking down this local guy and slapping the cuffs on him.

Jimmy was beside himself with anger and impatience. He wanted the dope out of his town, and he was at the point that he would do anything to get the job done. The briefing was to make his men aware that all other crimes were secondary to this, and they needed to keep that in mind at all times.

The only way they were going to get to this new guy was through his minions. They would have to arrest them and get them to talk. Otherwise, they would all be chasing their tails. His men were told to watch any Mexicans hanging on the streets. If they even appeared to be dealing, they needed a shakedown.

He dismissed his men and went into his office, where he wrote out the entire contents of the meeting for his own records. It helped him to remember, and it solidified things in his own mind. Just as he was finishing, his office door opened and Melody walked in. She looked as fresh as a ray of sunshine on a bouquet of flowers.

"Hey, baby-cakes!" She crossed the room and bent over, planting a long, languishing kiss on his lips. He moaned with pleasure.

When she pulled away, she said, "I have an appointment this morning. I stopped by to ask if you wanted to have lunch when I was done?"

"What time?" he asked.

She shrugged. "I don't know. Around 11:30?"

"Sounds good to me." He stood and put his arm around her and walked her to the door. "See ya then, lover."

"You bet!" She kissed him once again and left. He stood smiling like an idiot for a full two minutes before finally going back to his desk, and thoughts of cocaine.

∞

Kevin Marshall had obsessed over Jimmy O'Brien for days now. When he heard of the arrest of one of the street dealers he brushed it aside, but then he was told that the kid had squealed, and he had been sick over it. According to one of his men, the kid had been solid until O'Brien got a hold of him, then he had crumbled like a week-old cookie.

If Kevin Marshall had his way, he was going to kill that guy with his own bare hands, looking him in the eye the entire time and smiling.

But he had other things to worry about right now, and he had to force thoughts of O'Brien from his head. Tomorrow, Rodriguez's right-hand man, Manny Trujillo, would be there from Mexico. They had a meet planned at an abandoned ranch five miles outside of town. Only the top soldiers would be in attendance. The numbers were good, so Kevin wasn't worried. Trujillo was just coming to deliver some goods and look over operations.

He would likely show some concern about the Smith kid singing, but there was no way the cops could get to Rodriguez unless they got to Kevin, and they wouldn't get to Kevin unless the minions themselves sang. Trujillo would give them all a pep talk, which would ensure their silence. It would all be fine.

So, the meet was the next day at one o'clock in the afternoon. It would be brief and smooth, and then he could begin thinking about getting O'Brien once again.

∞

Jimmy walked into Mona's Café and immediately saw Melody. She was sitting in a booth looking out the window at the bright sunny day. She was a people watcher, and she loved to simply observe and take things in. It was something that Jimmy loved about his wife.

"Excuse me, ma'am, is this seat taken?"

Melody turned to him and smiled. "Not right now.

You are welcome to sit down, but once my husband gets here, he might get jealous."

Jimmy sat. "I think I could take him in a fistfight," he said. "Plus, I have a gun."

"Oh, well then you would certainly get the job done."

They both leaned across the table and kissed. "Thanks for meeting me for lunch, Jimmy."

"Any time, gorgeous," he replied.

They scanned the menu, and when the waitress brought their water, they gave her their orders. As soon as she left, Jimmy took Melody by the hand. "How did your appointment go? What was it for?"

"Well, that was why I wanted to have lunch," she replied cryptically. "It was a doctor's appointment."

Jimmy grew concerned. "Are you sick?"

Melody smiled. "No, Jim. I'm pregnant."

She said it so matter-of-factly that he almost didn't get it. It took him a full minute to respond, and when he did, he spoke a million miles an hour. "A baby? How far along are you? When did you make the appointment? How long have you suspected? Why the heck didn't you tell me?"

"Slow down, slow down," Melody said with a laugh as she held her hand in the air. "I didn't want to tell you before I knew for sure, you know? But I missed two periods so far; the doctor says I'm at eight weeks, and I have an initial ultrasound scheduled for two weeks from today if you want to go with me." She slid an appointment card across the table. "It's already in my calendar, so you can keep that for a reminder if you want."

Jimmy picked the card up and stared at it lovingly. "I'll keep it in a scrapbook. And of course, I will go with you, silly."

He paused, and tears began to well up in his eyes. "Melody, my life is perfect. It's all because of you, and I just want you to know that. You're my everything."

"And you are mine," she said in a husky voice.

Their food came then, but neither of them seemed able to eat. They began to make plans for a nursery, and they talked about baby boys and girls. They giggled and laughed like high schoolers when they talked about filling in her parents and Luciana and Matias.

Things for Jimmy O'Brien were just getting better and better.

CHAPTER 16

That evening two beat cops sat in the parking lot of Harver's grocery. It was eleven o'clock, and all was quiet. Their squad car was parked in the shadows and was barely visible from the street.

Keith Dowdry was sipping a hot coffee and eating a donut with colored sprinkles. His partner, Lymon Harris, ate a jelly donut. They both sat chewing in silence, surveying their surroundings. It was a peaceful night, and they expected nothing major on their shift.

Suddenly, from the right, a slight, younger Hispanic man began to stride up the sidewalk. He walked with a bit of a swagger, and even from where they sat, he appeared cocky and arrogant. He got to a Plexiglas bus stop and leaned against it. He looked up and down the road, then paused and lit a cigarette.

Suddenly a kid on a bike came riding up to him from the left. Harris dropped his donut and leaned forward. The squad car was already running, so he put himself in a position to take off if he had to.

The kid on the bike stopped and handed something to the Hispanic man. The man palmed off something in return, then the kid on the bike took off. The man started to swagger back in the direction he had come from. Dowdry began to call it in while Harris put the car in gear and punched it.

They were almost on him when the man took off running, but Harris didn't care. He slowed, and Dowdry jumped out and ran after him, and within minutes, he had the struggling punk cuffed and stuffed. They searched him and found what appeared to be an ounce of the good stuff, so they threw him in the back of the car and took him downtown for booking.

Once he was booked, they put him alone in an interrogation room and called the chief, waking him up.

"I know you don't wanna come down, chief, but we just brought in one of those minions. He had just under an ounce on him, and we're gonna put the pressure on," Harris told him.

Jimmy was already pulling up his pants. "No! You make him comfortable. Let him know you want to help him. I'll be there in twenty minutes, and I'll talk to him. Got it?"

"Yes sir."

They disconnected, and Jimmy put his shirt and socks on.

"Honey? What's going on?" Melody's tired voice cut through the darkness.

"Go back to sleep, dear," he said. "I'm just going in for a while to assist with the interrogation of one of these coke dealers. I'll be home in a couple of hours." He planted a kiss on her cheek, and she moaned her approval.

Within ten minutes, Jimmy was on the road to the station, and he was already mapping out his strategy for breaking the dealer's resolve.

∞

"So, what do you want to tell me?" Jimmy asked the young Hispanic man. "I can tell you that we can get the district attorney to go way easy on you if you help us."

The man, named Jose Torres, had some problems on his hands. Not only was he busted for dope, but he was illegal, and everyone knew what that meant. He had quite a bit to worry about at this point in time.

"If you cooperate, we can drop the charges for the coke," Jimmy told him. "You will be deported, but because there will be no charges on your record, you will still be able to get a green card. How old are you anyway, Jose?"

The kid looked down at his hands. "Twenty," he said.

"Twenty," Jimmy echoed. "Jeesh, Jose, you wouldn't be out of prison until you were forty. Can you imagine that? Twenty-plus years without tequila, cold cerveza, or any pussy at all. I can't imagine."

Jose was quiet. Jimmy knew he was thinking over what he had said, and he allowed him to do so. Finally, the young man said, "What you wanna know?"

"Who is the main man for Bernalillo?" Jimmy asked simply.

Jose looked him right in the eye. "I don't know his name. I know he is new, but I never meet him. I do know something, though."

"What do you know, Jose Torres?" Jimmy asked.

"I know that tomorrow they have a meeting, and one big guy will come from Mexico to see how things are going," Jose replied.

Jimmy stared at him; he was convinced the kid was telling the truth. "How do you know about this meeting?"

"We all know. They warn us to keep the ball rolling while it goes on," he said. "Only big guys go; not us street workers."

Jimmy leaned toward him. "Where is this meeting going to be held at, and what time?"

The kid shrugged and sat back. "There is a farm or ranch, that is left empty. It is like five miles out of Bernalillo, they are saying. The meeting is at that place. We are told they are unavailable from one o'clock 'til they contact us."

Jimmy only had to think for a fraction of a second. There was only one such place that he could think of: The old Chavez spread. Back in the day, it had been a very lucrative horse ranch, but Old Man Chavez sort of lost his mind when his wife died, and he let the place go to pot. Eventually, he died there, and his rotting corpse was found about five months after the fact. Due to that, no one had wanted to buy the place, and it had sat in a state of disrepair ever since.

He nodded at the boy. "This is good, Jose. This is very good. Now, we will take you to your cell to wait for the judge in the morning. I will tell the DA how you have helped. If the information you gave me is true, and it proves to be fruitful, you will get leniency; I guarantee it."

Jose looked relieved but scared. "Sir, you all will protect me from…"

Jimmy chuckled at him. "Now that, my boy, is out of my hands. You should have thought about all of that before you started selling drugs and ruining lives. See? You don't have to do the drugs for the drugs to take all you have away, now do you?"

He stood up and left the room, leaving the boy to cry. It didn't matter to him; the kid didn't care that the people of Bernalillo, as well as the rest of the world, were all on their knees because of this despicable drug. Why should he care about this kid? He wanted one thing, and he had received it.

Tomorrow at one. In the morning Jimmy would brief his men, and he would assign the officers who would accompany him in the raid. Jimmy wanted to see the whites of the eyes of the dirtball who was now running the drug trade in his town. He wanted the dirtball to see the whites of his as well.

He was pretty sure they would never forget each other after that.

∞

The security buzzer sounded loudly at Kevin Marshall's apartment around ten o'clock on the night before the meeting. He stood and walked over to the small security speaker and pressed the button.

A deep, gravelly voice with a Hispanic accent answered him. "Alejandro Trujillo."

Kevin didn't hesitate to press the button which unlocked the security door. It buzzed, and moments later, he heard a light tapping on the door to his apartment. He peeked out the hole in the door to see the tall, muscular Mexican with long hair and a goatee.

He opened the door and let Rodriguez's right-hand man enter the apartment. The two clasped hands and nodded before Kevin locked back up. "Sit down, man. You want a beer or a tequila?"

"Ah, tequila. Yes."

Kevin fetched the bottle, a small cutting board with knife and lemon, and salt, as well as two shot glasses. He sat in one of two black recliners with a black lacquered table between them.

"So, all is a go for the meet tomorrow," Trujillo said. They both did a shot, then he lit a cigarette and continued. "I will look over your records tonight, and that way when we get reports from the other men at the meet, we will know who is square and who is bullshit. Rodriguez will take no more bullshit. That is why he sent you. He sees you as a straight arrow. So do I."

Kevin nodded. "I couldn't be more ready. There are a couple of guys I am uneasy about. Not that I think they are stealing, but they are not doing their jobs. All they can think about is getting blow jobs and partying. They bring in their money, but it is the bare minimum, you know, man?"

"You think maybe they are sampling the wares?" Trujillo asked.

Kevin snorted. "I suspect, but as long as they bring

the right amount of cash, I say nothing. So far, so good."

Suddenly the phone rang. Kevin looked at the clock on the wall; it was damn near midnight. "Who the heck is calling me right now?"

"Might be Rodriguez, making sure I show up okay," Trujillo said.

Kevin picked up the phone. "This is Marshall."

"Sir, I think we have some small problem," the voice on the other line said.

"Who is this?" Kevin asked.

The man cleared his throat. "Antonio Acero, sir."

Acero was one of the men who were just under him. Not a street worker, but a supervisor of them. "What's happening, Antonio?"

"I sent Torres to run errands up at the grocery store," he said nervously. "He never came back. That was hours ago."

"Torres, huh?"

"Yes sir," the man replied.

Kevin thought for only a second. "Okay. Thanks. I will look into it."

He hung up the phone. Torres just happened to be one of the workers he was referring to when talking to Trujillo a few moments ago. The kid wasn't using the merchandise, at least Kevin didn't think so. But on two occasions he had come up short by five to ten dollars. Yeah, Kevin was sure he was using dope to get head, so he made the kid cover the loss with his own earnings. It was small enough of a discrepancy that Kevin didn't see a reason to jump the gun, but he was keeping his eye on the kid.

Now the kid hadn't returned from a run. That meant one of three things: he was either holed up with some bimbo, he was passed out drunk, or he was busted.

"Looks like one of the slackers I was talking about didn't come back from a run," Kevin said to Trujillo as he sat down and poured himself another shot.

Kevin nodded. "We have met, but he doesn't know my name, or even that I am the local boss. Anyway, he loves the ladies a bit too much. I suspect that is where he is."

Trujillo chuckled. "That pussy will sidetrack these chumps every time, yes?"

"Every damn time."

The two men toasted each other with their shot glasses and did their shots, then they resumed the conversation about the meeting the following day. There was going to be some serious talk about the workers getting their heads out of their asses. If they weren't going to step up, Kevin was going to oust them, and they could go back to Mother Mexico for all he cared. He wasn't about to lose his head because of some lazy worker bees. No way, not Kevin Marshall.

No, he would make sure their game improved, even if it meant them getting his size eleven foot in their bum. It was as simple as that. He was here to get things going like a finely oiled machine; Rodriguez expected that, and that was exactly what Rodriguez was going to get.

Kevin turned the television to CNN so they could watch a bit of the news along with their shots. It would help him wind down before going to bed. He needed a good night's sleep; tomorrow would be a very busy day.

R.W.K. Clark

CHAPTER 17

"Good morning, men. I hope all of you had either a restful weekend or a good night last night, because today is sure to present a challenge."

Jimmy greeted his men in the morning meeting with a sober look on his face and a serious tone. Today was the day that the men would be separated from the boys, and it would be done on both sides of the fence.

"As some of you may have heard, we have received inside information regarding cartel activity here in Bernalillo and in the surrounding area," he continued. "One of the cartel workers was apprehended, and during interrogation, he gave us pretty sound information regarding a meeting of the minor bosses, which is to be held at the old Chavez ranch just outside of town."

Some of the officers began to talk to each other in low murmurs. "Excuse me!" Jimmy held his hand up, and his tone was very sharp. "Now is not the time. You will have plenty of time to chat when I'm finished. Right now all of you need to be listening.

"We still have no idea who is running the show locally, but we do know that the main boss is none other than Pedro Rodriguez. Now, Rodriguez never gets his hands dirty with small town business, but I am confident he will send one of his trusted men to oversee things at the meeting. We can certainly count on our still unidentified local boss to be in attendance as well."

"The meeting is to take place at one o'clock this afternoon. We will be heavily armed, and we will be set up waiting long before they get there. There is a dune ridge running east to west along the property line, and all of us will be hidden there. Once the meeting begins, we will raid. Do you all understand?"

Everyone in the room nodded or answered verbally, and Jimmy was satisfied.

"I will head the operation. The team I want with me will be led by Art Vranish. Vranish, you will be backed up by a team of eight men. Those men are as follows: Strickland, Barber, Northrup, Abner, Lawson, Croft, Hackett, and Madera. Everyone got that?"

"Yes sir!" was the resounding response.

Jimmy nodded with satisfaction. "Good, good. Now, you need to be suited and armored up by o-nine-hundred-and thirty. We will pull out at o-ten-hundred hours, and we will all be solidly in place and ready to go by o-eleven-hundred at the latest. I know that it's two hours early, but preparation is more than required. We are finally at a place where we can make a nice, big, painful dent in this whole operation, and I expect this to go as smoothly as we make it.

"Remember: The meeting is supposed to begin at 1300 hours. Take the next few hours to prepare mentally and physically, whatever that means for you. We will car up at the given time, and we will pray together for guidance and protection before setting out; got it?"

Another round of 'Yes sirs' and Jimmy dismissed his men. Once he was alone, he gathered his paperwork, and after it was organized, he looked to the sky. "I'm gonna pray a bit now, God. You know how bad we need you today. Cover us, please. Get my men home safely to their families, and help me put a stop to the evil that is going on here. Amen."

Jimmy made his way back to his office, and as soon as he was inside, his telephone rang. He picked it up apprehensively, his nerves on edge. "Chief O'Brien."

"Hi, Jimmy." It was Melody, and he couldn't help but smile and sigh.

"Hi, baby. How are you feeling?"

"Good, I guess. My stomach is a bit upset," Melody said. "I'm not sure if it's the baby or the fact that you are diving head-first into terribly dangerous territory today."

Jimmy sat down at his desk. "It's my job, Mel. We talked about this incessantly before I ever proposed, remember?"

"I remember. I know, I know," she replied. "My head has it all together, it's just that my heart hasn't caught up."

"Well, I'm doing some praying, and it wouldn't hurt if you did as well," he said. "I'm going to be fine, babe. Have faith. If no one takes a risk, these guys will never be brought down. Can you imagine our baby growing up and doing this dope? No, I won't have it, Mel! I won't have it!"

"I know dear," Melody said. "I just wanted to let you know how much I love you, and I will be praying. Oh, I forgot to tell you last night. I got a call from Dr. Abrams. He said they had to move my ultrasound up; I'll be having it the day after tomorrow. If you can't go, I understand. It's short notice."

"Well, once this is over, I expect to be able to take a couple days with you and you alone. Let's plan on me going, but if not, make sure you bring some good pictures home, okay?"

Melody giggled. "Of course. I love you, Jimmy."

"I love you, Mel."

He hung up the phone and stared at it for a long time. He wanted to go, and he hoped all would be okay today. When he thought about the raid, his stomach gave a sick lurch. He was going to have to be very, very careful. No one in his life could afford for him to foul things up.

∞

Trujillo and Kevin sat at the kitchen table with steaming cups of coffee. It was 10:30 in the morning and Kevin's phone was ringing off the hook. There were to be ten men, all local under-bosses, who were to attend the meeting at one. To be sure they would all be in attendance, Kevin had directed them to call him, only identifying themselves by their last names. Trujillo would then check them off the list. So far only four men had called, but there was plenty of time.

They were to be at the ranch between 12:45 and 1. Being late was unacceptable, and they all knew it. They were to be prepared with written records and the current monies that were due. After the meeting, each of their supplies would be replenished, and they would be sent back out. Well, they would be sent back out if they weren't found to be lacking, that is.

Kevin got up and grabbed the coffee carafe, and he proceeded to warm up their cups. His mind went to Jose Torres. He had done some checking this morning with Jose's boss, and the guy still hadn't gotten any word on his whereabouts, nor had he heard from him. Either the guy had taken off, or he was sitting down at the jail. There was no way that Kevin, or any of the men for that matter, would call the jail. Instead, he had conferred with Trujillo right after the last call, and Trujillo, in turn, had called Rodriguez. The big boss had his means of finding out if any of his men had been collared, and he would do it without putting himself or any of his worker bees at risk. He would get back to them when he knew something; until then, they were to go on as planned.

So, the two men sat at the table going over what would be discussed at the meeting. Trujillo made sure he had all the dope ready to dole out to the workers at the end of the meeting. It was wrapped in plastic and stuffed in a large briefcase; enough for all the local troops for the time being. Kevin answered the phone whenever it rang, and each call resulted in a checkmark being made on the attendance list. They got so busy, in fact, that soon the call they were waiting for from Rodriguez completely slipped their minds.

The fact was that Rodriguez had connections. He had one guy locally that worked for him who was related to one of the officers in the Bernalillo Police Department. He was trusted implicitly by Rodriguez for two reasons: One, he was an older man in his forties; the cop was his younger brother. Two, he had been Rodriguez's employee for years, and to date, no one in his family had any suspicions regarding that employment. He pulled it off like an Oscar-winning actor.

Not to mention the fact that his little brother would come home from work and tell him all the good stuff. So, after Rodriguez got a call of concern regarding Torres from Trujillo that morning, he hung up the phone and dialed up his inside guy's number. Malcolm Abner, older brother to Danny Abner, one of the guys assigned to the raid, picked up the phone.

"Abner, it's Rodriguez. What do you know?"

Malcolm sat forward in his chair. "I was just going to call you, Rodriguez. I have something to tell you."

"Speak," Rodriguez replied simply.

Abner cleared his throat. "My kid brother left a while ago. I have been trying to find your number, but I think the paper I wrote the new one down on got thrown away. Anyway, he came home to eat an early lunch because they are assigned to a raid today." He glanced at the clock; it was 12:20. "The raid is to be held at Chavez Ranch, Rodriguez. A kid named Torres got collared, and he spilled the beans, man. All of the beans."

Rodriguez closed his eyes. His heart began to pound, but he remained calm. It was important to do that; now was not the time to panic. Now was the time for solid thinking.

"Okay," he replied. "I cannot talk any longer. I have to go and stop my men from going to the meet."

He hung up without waiting for a goodbye, and immediately he dialed Kevin Marshall's number. To his dismay, it rang and rang and rang. Finally, his fancy answering machine picked up.

"Son of a bitch!" Rodriguez screamed as he slammed the phone back into the cradle. He stood and began to pace, muttering obscenities in Spanish as he did.

Finally, he accepted it. He looked at his watch, shook his head, and sat back down. He knew he should have gotten them all pagers, but he didn't like them because they made his men look like drug dealers. After all, how many of these poor Mexicans really had the money for such a service, anyway?

Well, it was too late for regrets now. Rodriguez stared at the phone and braced himself. He fully expected to receive a call telling him all his Bernalillo men were busted. For someone who had so much power, he felt pretty damn powerless.

The first thing he would expect was for someone to sing. He was safe in Mexico, so he wasn't as concerned as he maybe should have been. He knew it wouldn't be Trujillo that was for sure. And he was pretty sure it wouldn't be Kevin Marshall. It would be one of the others, one of the street supervisors. Yes, it would be one of them.

He decided to worry about the priorities, and the main one was taking care of both Trujillo and Marshall. He would get them out if they were arrested. He would bring them south and keep them there, out of the reach of the long arm of the American law.

Rodriguez picked up his phone and dialed a number. "Carlos, we have a problem. I will need you to get over here to me right away, amigo."

He hung up the phone and sat back. There was absolutely nothing he could do now but wait.

CHAPTER 18

Chief Jimmy O'Brien and his men were positioned along the ridge, just like they had planned and been ordered to do. Each one was strategically placed; they had quickly gotten into position, and they silently waited for the men to begin showing up for the meeting below. From where they sat, they could see the old Chavez Ranch perfectly; it was as if they had front row seats to an insane cop movie.

The suspects began to arrive at twenty minutes before 1300 hours. The first car was a large SUV, and from what Jimmy could see with his binoculars, the thing was brand spanking new. It pissed him off that these mongrels were able to live in the lap of luxury at the expense of other people's lives.

Two men got out of the vehicle. One had long black hair and was obviously Hispanic. The other wore sunglasses and a baseball cap, but he was white. Jimmy deduced that these were the guys who were in charge and a jolt of electricity coursed through his veins. He couldn't wait to slap the cuffs on these so-and-sos.

Soon cars began to arrive one after another, a total of six in all. The first carried three men, the second two.

The next three each carried one apiece, and the final vehicle had two men. All six of the cars were old and beat up; none of them were shiny and new like the SUV. This confirmed what Jimmy already thought: the SUV held the guys in charge. The other men were the underlings, the street workers.

By one o'clock all was still.

Jimmy looked around at his men to see them all looking at him expectantly. "Okay, men," he said in a voice just loud enough for them to hear. "We'll go down, surround the place, and at my cue, we're busting in. I'll call it in first so the chopper can meet us. Got it?"

All of his men nodded, and Jimmy put his radio up to his face. "We're going downhill, copy?"

"Copy that."

They all rose and began the short trip down the ridge. Like the pros that they were, soon they were all in position, and they were all able to see Jimmy's face. He listened closely; he could hear voices from inside the ranch house, but he couldn't make out what was being said. He held up his hand and trotted forward a bit, then ducked down behind a large rock. He could suddenly hear what they were saying clearly.

"As you know, men, we have had a few of you who have slackers running our shit." This was the voice of the American, Jimmy was sure of it. It sounded a bit familiar, but the identification of the voice seemed to evade him, and he found that it made him a bit uncomfortable. "So, the first order of business today is to make one thing clear: shit rolls downhill. If you have someone not giving what is expected or more, you will be the one who is dealt with. I hope you are all getting me loud and clear."

Suddenly, the gravelly, deep voice of a Mexican broke through. "Which one of you is Acero?"

"Here, sir," replied a voice enthusiastically.

The gravelly voice continued. "Acero, have you had word on Torres?"

"No sir, I have not."

"Well, Rodriguez has been notified and is checking it out," the gravelly voice said. "We hadn't heard back from him before leaving, but whatever has happened to him, we will know soon enough. Let him and what happens to him be an example to all of you, and your men. Got that?"

∞

Jimmy turned to the team leader, Officer Vranish, and gave him a curt nod. All of the men suddenly ran forward, their automatic weapons poised and ready for action. They no sooner reached the front entrance than Vranish kicked it in and the men crossed the threshold like madmen escaping from the asylum.

Everyone in the room went for their guns without hesitation, and naturally, bullets began to fly, whizzing around like crazy. Jimmy ducked down behind a tattered sofa and peeked out over the top. That was when he recognized Kevin Marshall.

Kevin Marshall was the white guy who had been driving the SUV.

Kevin Marshall, the dirtball, was the Bernalillo boss.

Enraged, Jimmy came out from behind the sofa, spraying bullets as he went and screaming at the top of his lungs. He saw Kevin try to make a run for it, but a bullet tore through his upper left arm. He fell, a look of shock on his face. Jimmy began to focus on everyone else, shooting, shooting, and shooting some more. He felt two sharp slaps on his thigh and fell to the ground, crying out.

The shooting suddenly stopped as soon as it started. Jimmy looked around to see many of the 'underlings' lying on the floor, holding up their hands to show that they weren't armed. A few of them lay lifeless in pools of blood, but most were still breathing air. The long-haired Mexican that had arrived with Marshall lay dead on the floor, a bullet wound to his neck spraying blood, which was slowing down with each pump. His eyes were wide open, but Jimmy knew he didn't see anything anymore.

He turned to where Marshall had fallen to the floor, but he couldn't see him anywhere. "Where did the white guy go?" Just then he heard the helicopter and some sirens, and he assumed they would nab him outside. Right then he needed to worry about the arrests at hand.

An hour later, all of the living prisoners were cuffed and on their way to jail in town. Ambulances had the bodies of those who didn't make it out. Jimmy had asked about the white guy numerous times, but no one had seen any white guy. The SUV was still there, and it would be impounded, but Kevin Marshall was gone.

Jimmy was given powerful pain medication, then he

was transported to Bernalillo General for surgery. The fact that Kevin Marshall had been in the raid became a blur to him, and by the time he woke, it was the very last thing on his mind.

R.W.K. Clark

CHAPTER 19

When Jimmy woke after his surgery, he found himself in the recovery room surrounded by the three people he loved most in the world. His wife, Melody, his mother Luciana, and, of course, Matias Garcia, who was now his stepfather. According to them, the surgery was simply to remove two bullets that he had taken during the raid. He would be fine, though he would have to stay in the hospital for a couple of weeks. He would also have to use crutches at first when he was released, then he would graduate to a cane. Depending on how he did, he should be able to go back to work shortly after his release.

Regardless of all the good that had come out of the raid, Kevin Marshall was still on the loose. The police had yet to find out where he lived, but they did have one of the minor cartel members just about ready to give up some information that could lead to the discovery of his residence. It was only a matter of time.

On his fourth day in, Jimmy was lying in his bed watching an old rerun on television. His pain meds had him feeling a bit fuzzy, but he had slowly been tapering off, so he wouldn't have to endure that much longer.

He nodded in and out a bit, but would always jerk himself awake when he did.

Suddenly, the phone next to his hospital bed rang, making Jimmy jump.

He winced as pain shot through his leg, then slowly he reached for the receiver. "This is Jimmy."

"How are you, Jimmy? Long time no speak."

Jimmy sat up straight in bed, his eyes wide. Suddenly he was completely awake and alert. It was Kevin Marshall on the phone. Before he had a chance to respond, Kevin continued.

"You know, I swore to myself that I would get you, Jimbo," he said. "Ever since you saw to it that my ass was going away all them years ago. I have to admit, I had started to get over it. Until I saw you on the news when you became chief. Then it was suddenly like all the pain and anger were fresh, and I couldn't ignore it anymore. Not when you were right under my nose, fresh for the picking."

"Where are you, Kevin?" Jimmy asked in a low voice.

Now the man broke out in obnoxious laughter. "Like I would tell you!" He continued to laugh until eventually, it died down altogether. Jimmy listened to it through closed eyes, grimacing at the sound.

"Anyway, as for 'getting you back'; you should probably know I am in the process of doing so as we speak."

"What does that even mean, Kevin? You know, you're wasting your time running away. We are going to track you down, and you are going to either go to prison or die." Jimmy felt the rage growing inside of him.

Kevin chuckled once again. "Well, I'm sure. But for now, I have a little… shall we say… life insurance."

Jimmy didn't respond; he just waited for the bastard to go on.

"I have Melody. Pretty, pretty Melody."

Now Jimmy was shaking, and it sounded like alarms were going off in his head. The cocksucker had his pregnant wife! "You listen to me…" Jimmy began, but he was cut off.

"No! You listen to me!" Kevin was completely insane, and the instability could be heard in his voice. "I have Melody. If you want her back, I want to be able to get safely back to Mexico, no questions asked. I want no one to even try to lay a hand on me. Only when I am back down there will you find out where she even is, got it? You have three days!"

The phone went dead.

Jimmy wasted no time. He immediately dialed headquarters, and in a panicked rush told Officer Dan Abner what was going on. "You have to find out where he is; you have to help Mel, Dan!"

Dan promised to get right on it. Jimmy tried to get up, but as soon as his foot touched the floor, the severe pain blinded him. He immediately passed out into a crumpled heap.

∞

The next three days were spent locating Kevin Marshall. Jimmy was unable to play a part of any kind in the investigation or the rescue; the doctors kept him heavily sedated and strapped to the bed for his own good. But the Bernalillo Police were on it.

It turned out that one of the Mexican underlings had known where Marshall's apartment was all along. He had refrained from giving up the information because it would reveal that he had been sneaking around, following the local boss, and that could get him killed. The cops knew that he knew, though, and once they told him that Marshall was holding a pregnant woman hostage, the kid gave up the information easily. The last thing he wanted was to be charged with accessory to kidnapping or murder.

The police had surrounded building number 5336 at Pueblo La Casa Apartments. Three heavily armed officers broke into apartment 'A' and found Kevin Marshall holding a gun to the head of one Melody O'Brien. They were able to shoot him in the leg, saving Melody and disarming the man. He was arrested and taken in.

Kevin Marshall would not see the light of day again.

CHAPTER 20

"He has killed my right-hand man; he killed several of my men, and he has locked up the rest." Pedro Rodriguez was beside himself with anger and grief. He didn't know what to do, but he knew that he was going to have to deal with the son of a bitch American named Jimmy O'Brien. "I want this dealt with, but I don't want him dead; I want him to live to suffer through it, just as I must."

Malcolm Abner listened closely to the man. He could feel his grief, but he didn't know how to respond. "Pedro, I have a brother on the force, as you know. I do not want him to get hurt in any way over this."

"Malcolm, I will give you $100,000 to take care of this for me," Pedro continued. "Won't that be enough for Danny to turn the other cheek? Maybe even help?"

Malcolm thought about his father lying in bed in the other room. Cancer would take him; they had no money for the ongoing recommended treatment. When his father passed, his mother would soon follow, murdered by her own grief.

"Yeah, sure Pedro," he said finally. "I would. You have to give me time to talk to him, you know? What is it you want done to O'Brien?"

For the next ten minutes, Rodriguez outlined his vision of revenge to Malcolm Abner, and it sounded not only reasonable, but it also sounded fun and easy.

"We'll take care of it," Abner concluded.

He hung up the phone and took a deep breath. Right then his younger brother Danny walked into the room. He said nothing; he only held up a cordless telephone receiver.

He had been listening to the entire call.

"Danny, I…"

Danny held up his hand, signifying for his brother to stop. "There is nothing to say, Mal. At least, not for you." He crossed the room and sat down on the sofa. He stared at the phone in his hands and said, "It would keep daddy alive a little longer."

"Yes, Dan-o, it would."

"I'll take care of it, Mal. I know just what to do. Just be patient."

With that, Officer Dan Abner got up and left the room.

∞

Melody heaved her large, pregnant frame around to watch her husband as he prepared to leave for work. So much had happened in the last several months; he still walked with a cane, but he was doing so much better. She was proud of him and relieved that they all lived through the insanity.

He bent down and gave her a kiss goodbye, then limped his way out of the house and headed for the car.

Soon he was tooling down the road, his trusty cane leaning beside him on the passenger seat. "What would I do without you?" he asked, giving the wooden stick an affectionate pat.

Yes, he was back to work and in full swing of things. Kevin Marshall had pleaded guilty to his charges right away; he knew better than to prolong the inevitable. Just a week ago he was sentenced to life in prison; he was only waiting now to be transferred.

Melody was eight months along; she was having a good pregnancy in spite of all the insanity she had endured in the last few months. She was a tough woman, and he was proud to call her his wife. He couldn't wait to see their child, who they found out was a girl. They would be calling her Claire Elizabeth.

His mother and Matias were going to be relocating to Florida. His mother wanted to live by the ocean, and Mat was attracted to the idea himself. They were going to stay put until baby Claire came, of course. While they waited, Luciana spent a lot of time with Melody, and the two had become the very best of friends.

Jimmy parked his car in the lot, and grabbing his cane and briefcase, began to make his way into the station. On his way, many would stop to look at him. He would wave or say hello, but for some reason, he seemed to be getting a very distant response from each and every one of them. It was odd, and none of it escaped his notice. He blew it off, though, attributing it to the fact that it was early Monday morning.

Inside he got more of the same, and by the time he

reached his office, he was more than ready to shut the door behind him and get to work. As he turned the knob, he noticed that he had butterflies in his stomach, and he couldn't pinpoint why. Something was definitely... off.

He opened the door to find he had visitors. Seated in two of the chairs were police Commissioner Gordie Bradley and Mayor Suzanne Lloyd. Both of them sat stiffly, their eyes shifting to and fro. They were not smiling; as a matter of fact, both of them looked a bit disgusted.

"Wow," Jimmy said with a smile. "To what do I owe this great pleasure?"

"Shut the door, Jim," Bradley said.

Jimmy knit his brow, the smile fading from his face, and closed the door behind him. "What's going on, Gordie?"

"Sit down, Jimmy." This came from the mayor, and her voice was very curt.

He took a seat and propped his cane on his desk. "So, I'm sitting. What the heck is this about?" He saw that his secretary had made him a pot of coffee, so he grabbed the carafe off the small stand next to his desk and filled his cup. He took a long drink as his question was answered.

"Yesterday we received an anonymous call," Gordie began. "The caller said that you had been stealing, and using, cocaine, from the evidence locker for some time."

"What? I don't know what you are talking about!"

Jimmy was getting angry now. This had to be some kind of sick joke. "I have never used drugs in my life, Gordon!"

The commissioner shrugged. "And that is what we believed. Until your office was shaken down at 5:30 this morning." He held up an evidence bag, which had already been tagged and clearly marked. It held at least two ounces of the treacherous white powder. "But this was found in your desk."

Jimmy was livid. He drained his coffee and threw his cup at the wall, causing it to shatter on impact. "You have to be kidding me!"

"No, Jim. We're not," Gordie concluded.

Suzanne sat forward now. "Jimmy, we're going to need you to give us a urine sample to be tested right away."

"Absolutely!" He grabbed his cane and struggled to stand. "Let's do this thing, right now!"

Gordie and Suzanne stood as well. "You know, this will rule out usage, but the possession charge will still have to be faced. And I'll have to supervise the drop for the urinalysis. I'm sorry, Jim."

Jimmy waved him off and went into his private bathroom, with Gordie on his heels. The commissioner had a cup in his hands, as well as a foil packet containing a cocaine stick test. Jimmy knew them all too well. It would be a matter of minutes before he was cleared, of usage anyway.

As he stood and pissed in the clear plastic cup, his mind reeled. What the heck was going on here, anyway?

He was in shock, stunned by the accusations that faced him. Now he understood all the strange looks he got on the way in. Now it was making a bit more sense.

All he knew was that someone was setting him up.

He handed the cup over to the commissioner, then stood behind him and watched as the man dipped the stick into his urine. He wasn't going to move a muscle until this was over. For all he knew, Gordie and Suzanne were the ones setting him up. Nope, he would keep his eyes on everyone.

He had worked his entire life for this. He had focused and sacrificed. He had done the right thing, and it had cost him his youth, a social life, all of it. Now here he stood, accused of stealing evidence and doing drugs, and the burden of proof was literally going to be on him, no matter what anyone said.

He watched and waited for what seemed like a thousand years, but all of his vigilant watching made no difference. The test showed two red lines: Dirty. His urinalysis was positive for cocaine.

"That can't be right..." he muttered. He was dumbfounded.

Gordie quietly replied, "You see it for yourself, Jim."

The man rapped on the bathroom door twice, and sure enough, two uniformed officers who had been friends with Jimmy for years stepped into the bathroom and slapped the cuffs on him. One patted him down while the other asked, "Do you have anything sharp, or any drugs, Chief?"

Jimmy could only shake his head. His mouth was

hanging wide open in shock. One of them grasped him by the arm to support him while the other carried his cane. The commissioner and the mayor followed behind.

All of the officers seated at their desks watched as Chief Henry James O'Brien was led away to the jail to be booked and face the charges.

∞

Officer Danny Abner watched as Jimmy was led away. He kept a look of grief on his face, but he couldn't be feeling better. Once they were out of sight and the others began their muttering and gossiping, he stood and made his way out of the station. He went to his car and drove straight to the pay phone booth at the In and Out station. Once inside the booth, he emptied all of the change in his pockets onto the metal surface that served as a tiny desk.

He dialed a number that was located in Mexico, Juarez to be exact. A mechanical voice came on and told him to deposit five dollars for the first minute, or ten for a five-minute call. Danny Abner deposited ten dollars in change and listened as the phone began to ring.

The person he was calling picked up after the very first ring. "This is Rodriguez."

Danny cleared his throat. "It is finished. He has been arrested, and he even tested positive for the drug."

Laughter filled his ears, but he did not join in. Abner couldn't even smile. What he had just done was wrong, so very wrong. But now he could keep his father alive for a while longer. Maybe they could even kick cancer altogether.

Once Rodriguez stopped laughing, he became all business. "One of my men will be bringing a case of the money we agreed upon. He will be at your home in three hours or so; he is coming from Albuquerque. And Dan, thank you for your help. You will certainly not regret it."

Danny looked at the ground, his eyes filling with tears. "No, I'm sure I won't. Thanks, Mr. Rodriguez."

He hung up the phone and stared at it in disgust for a long time. The words of Pedro Rodriguez echoed sickly in his ears. 'You will not regret it.'

He already did…

CHAPTER 21

Former Bernalillo Chief of Police Jimmy O'Brien sat in the back of the sheriff's transport vehicle staring somberly out the window. He wore cold, hard handcuffs and shackles. His attire consisted of bright orange scrub pants and a matching scrub top. His hair was a greasy mess.

His pride kept him from admitting to something he didn't do. Plea bargain? Never, he had no other choice. His mother didn't even believe he was innocent, and she begged him to take a plea so he wouldn't shame Melody any more than he already had. He couldn't blame Luciana; after what his father had done, she thought the accusations against Jimmy were no surprise.

Melody had written and visited him while he was in jail, but once he was sentenced and got thirty years, she was done. The last letter he received told him to go on with his life because she was going to go on with hers. It also said he would be receiving divorce papers in the mail, and she begged him to sign them without putting up a fight. After all, once baby Claire came, she didn't want the girl living with this kind of shadow over her life. She promised to tell the child that he had been killed in an accident to save face for him, but she didn't want him to ever try to make contact with his own daughter.

"Just stay out of our lives." That was the last line in the letter.

Now he was riding in the transport vehicle on his way to the Penitentiary of New Mexico. He was terrified. After all, he had been a cop, and criminals hated cops. That was the least of his concerns, though. Penitentiary of New Mexico was where all of the men were housed that he had busted, including Kevin Marshall.

He closed his eyes to stop tears from flowing and leaned his head back on the seat.

The Sheriff's Deputy began to razz him. "How does it feel to be on the other side of the fence?"

Jimmy didn't answer him, so the guy continued. "Tell me, how does someone with a life like yours crumble and cave under the pressure of some damn drug, anyway? Talk about throwing it all away! You make me sick."

Jimmy still didn't answer. Instead, he let himself go completely into his mind, to a time when he was young and was dreaming dreams of the *Men in Blue*.

He thought about how determined he was, and how carefree. It had been so important to him to do the right thing and be the right person that he had never considered the fact that sometimes the bad guys win. No, many times the bad guys win.

It had all been for nothing.

At the exact same time that the sheriff's deputy had begun to razz Jimmy O'Brien, Melody was hit hard by her first labor pain.

She waited, and she timed them, and when she saw that they were consistent and growing closer together, she called Mat and Luciana Garcia. They would be right there, they assured her; practice her breathing exercises and relax. They would take care of everything once they arrived.

She thought about Jimmy only briefly, then she pushed him out of her pain-stricken mind. He didn't deserve to be considered; after all, he had obviously had no consideration for her. She despised him now more than she had ever loved him.

∞

They were closer now, Jimmy and the deputy. A sign loomed large ahead, and Jimmy read, "Santa Fe... 32 miles; Penitentiary of New Mexico... 23 miles". Then "WARNING: Do NOT pick up hitchhikers; Prison ahead." Jimmy couldn't help but snicker, and it made him sick.

"What the heck are you laughing at? You have so much that you should be finding funny at this point in your miserable life, don't you?" The deputy was a nasty man, full of himself and self-righteous. Jimmy got control of his laughter and continued to look out his window as the tears fell freely and silently from his eyes.

Right then, as the deputy was yelling at him yet again, Melody was sitting in the backseat of Mat and Luciana's car. Her pains were wracking her body. Luciana was in the back seat with her, helping her to focus and breathe. Her mother-in-law had gone to Lamaze with her, and she would be her birth coach. For that Melody would be eternally grateful.

∞

They pulled up to the massive fence in the transport vehicle. Jimmy saw that it was flanked by two guard shacks, both of them occupied by armed prison officers. The deputy rolled his window down, and one of the guards leaned in.

"What do you have?"

The deputy snickered. "Well, I've brought 'Cocaine Cop' to you. I'm sure you've been waiting."

The guard peered into the back seat and grinned. "Waiting? Heck, every inmate in this place has been on the edge of their steel bunks with anticipation!" The guard began to laugh, and the second guard, who was standing on the passenger side of the car, joined in with gusto.

They waved the vehicle through, telling the deputy, "Just take him into Intake in Building A. They'll have you sign some papers of release, and then they'll take it from there."

The deputy did as he was instructed, pulling his vehicle into a sally port which was attached to Building A. He removed Jimmy from the car, and making sure he had all of the paperwork he needed, he pushed the stainless steel button on the wall next to the heavy metal door. It buzzed horribly loud, then after a deafening clang, the door slid open.

Just as the door began to shut, Jimmy turned around; he could barely see the tops of the green trees as the door began to close.

∞

Right at that moment, Melody gave one final push, and Claire Elizabeth O'Brien came screaming into the world.

∞

Seconds later the metal Penitentiary door slammed shut.

ENTREATY

This book was made possible by reviews from readers like you. Reviews fuel my creativity. If you enjoyed this novel, I implore you to please write a review and share your experience on the retailer's website. The livelihood for authors is entirely dependent on reviews, and I must say, it is the largest obstacle as a struggling author that I have encountered. Please tell a friend, tell a loved one about this read. With your help, I will be one step closer to overcoming this obstacle. In return, I thank you from the bottom of my heart, and sincerely appreciate your time and effort.

Humbled, with gratitude,

R.W.K. Clark

ABOUT THE AUTHOR

I am a father of two beautiful children, Jon and Kim. They are my motivating forces; they are the lighthouse in this vast ocean. In my life, they are the air that I breathe; they are the oasis in this desert of uncertainty. They are my greatest joy in life and my number one priority. I have a long list of hobbies, and I attribute that to my lust for life! I like to surround myself with positive people, who share the same interests. Family values, the arts, outdoors, nature, and travel are tops on my list. I embrace attending cultural and artistic events because I believe dramatic self-expression is the window to the soul. I wear my heart on my sleeve, and I still believe in chivalry, and I always treat people the way I want to be treated.

www.rwkclark.com

www.ingramcontent.com/pod-product-compliance
Lightning Source LLC
Chambersburg PA
CBHW030305180626
46810CB00003B/917